Me & My Hittas
By
Tranay Adams

Me & My Hittas

Me & My Hittas/ Tranay Adams-1st ed. © 2016

ISBN: 978-1-7377789-1-2

Email: dopereadzpresents@gmail.com

Facebook: Tranay Adams

Instagram: Tranay Adams

Cover Artist: DIVINE

Publisher: Dope Readz Presents

Prologue

He sat on the hood of his silver Monte Carlo SS taking pulls from a blunt laced with marijuana and crack cocaine. His head was hidden beneath his blue hood, which he wore under a black leather coat. His eyes were bloodshot and glassy, filled with hurt and animosity. His cheeks were wet and slick from crying. Big teardrops fell from his eyes hitting the asphalt and the toe of his Air Max sneaker. He wiped his face with the sleeve of his leather coat. He continued to take puffs of his blunt until half of it was gone. He then grabbed the bottle of Jack Daniel's and cracked it open. He took the bottle to the dome, guzzling the dark liquor thirstily and glancing at the picture of his younger brother, Dizzy. More tears fell, hitting the picture and rolling off of it. He continued to drink; in between doing so he talked with his brother. Although he had left this life for the next, he heard Dizzy in his ear.

"Niggaz done me foul, straight up dirty," He heard Dizzy loud and clear, "You seen me at the morgue? Shit split all open; a nigga gone have to have a closed casket funeral.

"Who did it, bro? Tell me and I'ma leave them pussies wet. That's on everything." Reboc swore, taking a pull from the blunt and then guzzling the Jack.

"The Slobs," Dizzy spoke in his ear.

"Who?

"Nigga, all of 'em, they supposed to be at that Demos game." Reboc looked to Jefferson's High School's football field where people were standing out waiting for the football players to emerge. "Avenge me, bro, do for me what I can't do for myself!"

"Don't even trip, I got chu; these niggaz 'bout to feel some hot shit." He guzzled more of the Jack and wiped his mouth with the back of his fist. He reached into the passenger side window and sat the bottle down in the *passenger seat. He then continued with the consumption of the laced blunt.*

"Dead all of them niggaz, Cuz, all of 'em." Dizzy urged him.

"Don't worry about nothing, bro bro, big bruh got chu...Always." Reboc replied, holding the smoke in his lungs. He looked up and saw a horde of people coming off of the football field. He spotted more than a handful of them in red clothing. For him they were as good as Bloods; the same Bloods that aired out his kid brother. This angered Reboc and he saw through a haze of red. His nostrils flared and he clenched his teeth so tight that you could see the skeletal bone structure of his jaws.

Reboc dropped his blunt on the ground and mashed it out under the heel of his Air Max. He walked around to the trunk of his Monte Carlo and popped it open. He reached inside and when he withdrew his hand back he was gripping an Ingram. Next, he checked the magazine to make sure that it was loaded. He smacked it back into its slot and cocked the hammer on it. After slamming the trunk closed, Reboc stepped upon the curb to handle his business.

***

The locker room was in an uproar. The Demos had just won the championship game. The players were dancing around and acting a fool. Blips! Sounded off throughout the crowded room as the corks of champagne were being popped; none of the players were old enough to drink but the coach had made them all promise to keep it as their little secret.

"Alright, alright, quiet down!" Coach Roosevelt held up the football and the locker room fell to silence. He was a copper complexioned gent with salt and pepper hair that he wore in a close fade. He was dressed in a worn baseball

cap and a blue Polo shirt. A whistle hung from his neck down over his chest. His eyes scanned the locker room as he held the pig skin in the air while his free arm lay draped over the quarter back's shoulders. "Now you guys played one hell of a game out there, you crushed your opponents like they were roaches. You went out there and dominated...You conquered...You whipped those guys asses and proved that you were the better team. You're warriors, gladiators, each and every one of you," he pointed the football around at the players surrounding him.

"Now, you all did your thing out there tonight, but there was one of you out there that stood out just that much more. His proficiency and execution out there was stunning, so it's only right that I present him with the winning game ball..." he looked to the brown skinned kid that was under his wing and smiled, as he chewed gum.

"Here you go, son." he passed him the football and the kid beamed brightly.

"Everyone, let's give a round of applause for Tramel." The coach clapped along with the players. Two of the offensive linemen lifted Tramel over their heads and paraded him around the locker room with everyone hooting and hollering. A smile stretched across the M.V.P's face.

*****

"Ma, it's taking Mel forever and a day to come out here," Killa Dre spoke of his big brother. His thin dread locks were spilling from underneath an oversized Pirates snapback, lying over his shoulders and back. He had smooth brown skin and dark eyes. His baby face and slight mustache lead you to believe that he was younger than his seventeen years.

If Tramel was an angel then, Killa Dre was definitely a devil. The boy treaded down the path of his father before him. Cutty Johnson was a street veteran that earned his keep extorting hustlers and working as a hired gun. His exploitation of the streets came back to haunt him when he put the muscle on the wrong nigga'z brother and got his top blown the fuck off. After his death his youngest son dove headfirst into the street life, sticking his hands into some of everything illegal to earn a dollar. When drama came his way he murdered it on the spot, which garnered the young hitter the alias, Killa Dre. The boy's mother did all she could to stop him from becoming just another statistic, but she was too late, he was too far gone. The streets had him and she wasn't letting go. So the little nigga'z mother poured all of her attention into her oldest son, encouraging him to follow his dreams of playing pro football in the N.F.L.

"Give 'em a second, baby, I'm sure he'll be out in a minute." Tramel and Killa Dre's mother said. She and her youngest stood amongst the crowd waiting for the players to exit the locker room. She trembled slightly and rubbed her arms trying to keep warm.

"Ma, you want my jacket?" Killa Dre asked, seeing his mother struggling to keep warm.

"Nah, I don't want chu to catch a cold, I'll be alright." She responded, rubbing her arms harder and faster to keep warm.

"Ma please, I'ma grown man, I can brave this weather." He removed his leather jacket and draped it over her shoulders. He then pulled her under his arm and smiled. Rebecca looked up at her youngest and smiled, too. Her and her boys were a close knit family.

"Thank you, son."

"You're welcome, ma."

The doors of the locker room opened and the players expelled into the crisp, cold air. The air felt cooler than usual against the players' skin since they'd taken showers before they came outside. Tramel and his team mates moved to greet their loved ones. Tramel was wearing a red Atlanta Hawks snapback cocked to the right with a matching jersey. A thin gold necklace and cross lay upon his chest.

"Hey, momma," Tramel kissed his mother on the cheek and embraced her lovingly.

"That was a good game you and your team played, y'all tore them boys up." His mother stated proudly.

"Thanks, ma," Tramel grinned. He slapped hands with Killa Dre, "What's up, baby boy?"

"You did your thang out there tonight."

"We did our thang out there tonight; I ain't nothing without my team."

"That's right, son, stay humble, don't never let any of this go to your head."

"I won't, ma, I promise."

"Can you do me a favor?" she asked him. Tramel threw his head back 'like what's up?' "Turn the volume down on that jersey, it's too loud."

She narrowed her eyes into slits and held a hand above her brow, pretending to be blinded by the color of his jersey.

"You're a regular standup comic tonight." He smirked.

"What's that?" Killa Dre pointed to the pig skin gripped in his big brother's hand.

"Coach Roosevelt blessed me with the winning game ball."

"Let me see it." Tramel tossed Killa Dre the football.

"Go long, Mel." He gripped the football with both hands.

"Hold my bag for me, ma." Tramel gave his mother his Nike duffle bag and darted towards the street.

"Tramel, Dre, y'all be careful." She yelled out as Tramel darted into the street looking for his brother to launch the ball.

Killa Dre threw up a Hail Mary. The football went high into sky and came down like a nuclear warhead. Tramel caught the football. He put his hand behind his head, stuck out his tongue, and did a funny dance in the middle of the street, moving his hips in a circular motion with the football outstretched.

Killa Dre and their mother laughed.

Killa Dre cupped his hands around his mouth and yelled out, "Throw it back, foolie!"

"Alright," Tramel yelled back. He took a stance and gripped the football, prepared to let it fly. He cocked his hand back and threw his arm forth, releasing the football.

***

Through bloodshot and glassy eyes, Reboc watched the horde of people spill out of the school and head towards their vehicles. The men and women in red clothing stood out to him the most. His eyes locked onto a caramel skinned kid in a red Atlanta Hawks snapback and matching jersey. The kid had darted out into the street and spun around. He caught a football and took a stance to throw it back. At that moment Reboc heard his brother in his ear again "He's one of them, bro, I remember his face! Kill'em!" Reboc's face twisted into a murderous scowl. He became so angry that the haze of red returned before his sight. His brother's voice enticed him to claim a body, a few of them. "Kill'em all!" his brother egged him on.

Reboc brought his Ingram into play, lifting and pointing it at the kid in the Atlanta Hawks fit. He squeezed the trigger of his weapon and slugs spat mercilessly from the barrel, sending heat in the kid's direction.

***

Boof!

The football exploded and hit the ground.

A look of surprise took Tramel's face and he mouthed, "What the fuck". He looked to the ground at the football wondering what happened to it. He looked to his right and bullets rushed him, slamming into his torso and chest. The searing pain the sizzling metal brought caused his face to contort with excruciation. His eyes narrowed into slits and he looked up trying to see who his shooter was. Before Tramel's eyes could register the gunman, half of his face was blown off and his form was smacking down on the street.

"Noooooooo," Killa Dre and Tramel's mother screamed, after witnessing her oldest son being mowed down by a hail of bullets. The wail of her voice snatched Reboc's attention from Tramel's body and he went to point his Ingram in her direction when a blur of a person shot by him. He swung his weapon around and sent a line of fire at the blur's back, dropping him in the middle of the street.

By this time the streets were in chaos and pandemonium with people running every which way, trying to avoid some hot shit. Reboc waved his Ingram around, dropping the bodies of the people that tried to run. The screams and cries of his victims made his dick hard. A satanic smile stretched across his face and he licked his lips, continuing to release his hell on earth. When Reboc's Ingram clicked empty, he ejected its magazine and checked it. Seeing that the cartridge was spent, he reached into the pocket of his leather coat to retrieve another one. He smacked the fresh magazine into his weapon and cocked it. He went to finish his reign of terror when he heard the wail of police cars sirens zooming in his direction. He ignored the sirens and let off two more sprays. Having dropped two more bodies, he retreated for his vehicle.

***

Killa Dre and his mother were hunched down behind a parked car. He'd ushered her there when the shots went off that claimed Tramel's life.

7

"We've got to see about your brother." She told him as tears dripped from her eyes. Her heart was wreaking havoc inside of her chest and she was damn near hyperventilating.

"Okay. I'll check it out, you stay here." Killa Dre told his mother. She nodded her head. He looked over the trunk of the car through the back window and saw Reboc running in his direction.

"Shit!"

"What's wrong?"

"He's coming!"

"Oh, God."

There wasn't any time for Killa Dre and his mother to run without drawing Reboc's attention and possible gunfire. Realizing this, the young nigga pulled his mother behind him and prepared to use his body as a human shield. He'd die protecting the life of his mother if need be.

Killa Dre frowned and clenched his teeth. His jaw twitched with tension as he prepared for what was to be his fate.

In what seemed to appear as slow motion, Reboc ran past Killa Dre and his mother's hiding place. He pulled his hood from off his head and gave Killa Dre a side profile. Once the young nigga had gotten a good look at the side of Reboc's face, it seemed as if time had sped back up again, like in the movie "300". Once Killa Dre saw Reboc smash out, he and his mother rose to their feet. They surveyed their surroundings and found bloody bodies scattered throughout the street. Other survivors emerged from out of their hiding places and moved to check on their loved ones that were lying twisted in the sttreet. Sobs and screams filled the air once the survivors came to the realization that their loved ones had been murdered.

When Killa Drew and his mother saw Tramel lying in the street with red streams flowing from him, they took off running in his direction.

***

As soon as Reboc bent the corner at the end of the block, he slowed his ride down to a moderate speed and sat his warm weapon down on the passenger seat. When Reboc pulled his hand back after laying his Ingram down on the passenger seat, he noticed that there were specks of blood on it. He pulled a blue bandana from the inside of his leather coat and wiped the specks of blood from his hand, stuffing it back inside of its hiding place. He then picked up his cell phone and scrolled through the contacts until he found the number that he was looking for. Seeing Nightmare he tapped the screen, placing the call and bringing the cell to his ear. He was high out of his mind and needed assistance disposing of his ride and finding a place to lay low for a while.

***

Nightmare, Nike and Supacrip kicked it inside of his garage passing a smoldering blunt around and discussing hood shit.

"That nigga Reboc fucked up behind his bro bro, Cuz." Nike announced, "That nigga howling for real."

"True dat," Supacrip cosigned. "He was in the middle of the street getting shit faced and letting that thang go in the air the other night. He told me and this nigga if he doesn't find out who slept Dizzy, then he's gone ride on all of our enemies until he feels better. The homie done lost it. We need to holla at him before he goes off the handle and does some kamikaze type shit."

"I figure the best way to shut him up is to either kill him or give him an enemy to ride on." Nike said.

"Well, we can't kill the homie, that's Miss Graves' last living child." Nightmare took the blunt from Nike. "He wants a killa for his brotha? Then we'll find him one."

"Yeah, but who?" Nike asked.

"Whoever we choose it's gotta be a real head busta." Supacrip chimed in. "A fool that's known for splitting niggaz' wigs."

Nike and Nightmare nodded in agreement.

"I'll think of someone." Nightmare took a pull from the blunt and expelled white smoke. Just then his cell phone rang. He dipped into his pocket and pulled it out. A picture of Reboc and his number was on the screen. He tapped the screen to answer it and placed the cell phone to his ear. "What's cracking, Cuz? Shit, pull into the alley behind the house." He hung up and slipped the cell phone back into his pocket.

"What's happening, Cuz?" Supacrip asked.

"What's the deal?" Nike inquired.

"Reboc done got himself into some shit. Come on, that nigga rolling up through the alley."

***

"Noooooo, oh, God, not my baby, not my child," Killa Dre and Tramel's mother wailed at the top of her lungs. Her individual braids hung loosely over her face and sprawled over her shoulders. Her chocolate cheeks were slicked wet with tears and green snot oozed from her nose. The Demos jersey she wore was identical to Tramel's and was splotched with his blood. He lay at her side. She held his limp hand in one hand while she used the other to caress it. Half of Tramel's face was blown off and a chunk of his head was missing. The pain and horror he met before his death was etched on face.

Killa Dre was on his knees on the opposite side of his older brother. He stared at Tramel's mutilated face as tears cascaded down his cheeks. The tears seemed to come nonstop but he tried to keep himself from breaking down like his mother. He knew that he'd have to be the stronger of the two. With his brother and father gone, he'd have to step up to the plate and be the man of the house now.

A hand grasped Killa Dre's shoulder. He looked up and saw a police officer there. He knew that his time had been cut short with his brother and that it was time to say goodbye. Killa Dre gave the police officer a nod and he left him be. He then whispered something into Tramel's ear and kissed him on the temple. He got to his feet and helped his mother to hers. She embraced him tightly, sobbing into his chest. Killa Dre rubbed her back soothingly and watched as a white sheet was draped over Tramel's body. His blood quickly spotted the sheet red. At that moment, Killa Dre knew that his life would never be the same. From that night forward he wouldn't rest until vengeance was his.

***

Reboc sat on the end of Nightmare's bed, staring up at him as he straightened out the collar of his shirt. Once Nightmare had finished straightened out his homie's collar, he smoothed out the wrinkles in his shirt. He then cupped Reboc's face in his hands and stared into his bloodshot and glassy eyes. Nightmare pressed his forehead against his

homeboy's and held it there for a second. "I love you, Cuz." Reboc said it back. Nightmare kissed his forehead and turned around to Bobby Blue. She was at the opposite end of the bed snapping closed the locks of some luggage.

"You got everything in there?" Nightmare asked.

"Yeah, the whole kit and caboodle," Bobby nodded.

"Good."

"Yo," Reboc stole Nightmare's attention, holding the blunt up to his face.

Nightmare received the cough medicine and took a few puffs that made white smoke clouds surround him like he had appeared out of thin air.

"Bobby, hit up Nike and see what's taking him and Supa so fucking long." Nightmare said before taking a pull from the blunt.

"We're here."

Nightmare turned around to find Nike and Supacrip standing in the doorway.

"Y'all dumped that M.C and set it on fiya?" Nightmare asked.

"Yep," Nike answered. "Help me grab Reboc's shit so we can scram, Supa." Nightmare packed some of his own clothing for his comrade to wear during his time away.

Nike and Supacrip grabbed Reboc's luggage and headed out of the door, leaving the men to themselves.

"Where you setting me up at, Cuz?" Reboc asked.

"My big sis's crib."

"Shantel's spot? Aint that in The Jungle?"

"Yep, don't worry about it though, you're straight." Nightmare assured him. "Her baby's daddy, Tay Rock, is a reputable over there, and he assured me that you're in good hands. I'm laying a few racks on him to guarantee that."

"Still, I'm not feeling The Jungle." Reboc took the Jack Daniel's bottle to the head. He brought the bottle down and wiped

His lips with the sleeve of his leather coat.

"Me neither. But it's the best I could do on such short notice. Just lay low a couple of weeks over there until shit blows over and I'll send for you."

"Alright, Cuz."

"Gimmie some love, man." Nightmare opened his arms.

Reboc sat his bottle Jack Daniel's bottle down beside the bed and embraced his brother from another with a gangsta hug. Afterwards, he broke their embrace and picked the Jack Daniel's bottle back up. He gave Nightmare dap and staggered out of the bedroom.

Nightmare hung his head and massaged the bridge of his nose. Bobby approached him from the rear, rubbing his back.

"Are you alright, daddy?" she asked.

He nodded and said, "I'ma thousand."

Chapter One

A month later

Killa Dre lay back behind the wheel of his Dodge Charger, blowing smoke from his nostrils, eyes hooded from the exotic weed. He sat up in his seat having been zapped back from the night that his brother had been murdered in cold blood. His recalling was so real that he patted himself down and looked around to make sure he was where he last remembered. Garnering looks from his homeboys, Woo and Big Head, he sighed with relief and silently thanked God that he was in one piece.

Killa Dre had been fucked up ever since the day he lost his big brother, Tramel. All he did was play football, talk to girls and work his part-time job at Jon's Market. He was a nice kid with a good head on his shoulders. Everybody in the neighborhood had love for him; they just knew he was headed for N.F.L stardom. When he wasn't playing football, you could catch him with some of the neighborhood kids tossing a pig-skin around. He didn't gangbang, but that didn't stop someone from staining the streets burgundy with his blood.

As Tramel lay dead in him and his mother's arms, Killa Dre promised him that he'd bring his killer to justice, street justice. He vowed to never stop until he murdered the crip that killed him; even if it meant he'd be lying in a grave beside him when it was all over. Tears threatened to spill down the young nigga'z cheeks as thoughts of his late brother stirred up emotions inside of him. Not wanting his homeboys to see him so vulnerable, he shut his eyes for a moment and drew the tears back in.

"You straight, my nigga?" Woo asked before sucking on the end of a blunt. He was a tall cat with dark caramel skin and hazel green eyes. He wore a short unkempt afro that always had a red pick in it. Woo was a dangerous fella who lived his life by the gun.

"Yeah," he nodded, feeling the fog rise from his brain. His high was coming down having relived that experience. Taking a deep breath, he ran his hand down his face and exhaled.

"You sho'?" he raised an eyebrow.

"Yep."

Woo took a couple of puffs from the blunt and smoke wafted around the confines of the vehicle. After his indulgence he passed that shit to the back where that nigga Big Head was perched, watching the streets from the back window.

"Yo, Big," he passed the blunt to the little nigga in the backseat.

Big Head leaned forward and took it from between his homie's pinched fingers. Big Head was a short, big head nigga that wore his kinky hair in a Mohawk. He was lethal behind the trigger, but what he really loved to do was fight. He held the title of Knock-Out King on his block, successful laying out niggaz twice his size. The little dude was like a wild pit bull when set loose from its chain, ready to get it in. His record was thirty-four and owe. He was with the shit wherever, whenever for whatever reason.

Big Head was about to take a pull from the blunt when he noticed that it was wet at the end. He frowned and pulled out a Bic lighter of his own. "Damn, Blood, you done wet the mothafucka all up!"

"So what?" he flipped the sun visor down, scowling at him through the rectangular mirror.

"So what? Nigga, I don't know who's pussy them big ass lips been sucking on."

"They been sucking on yo' mammy's nigga," He chuckled and nudged Killa Dre who gave a half hearted smile. Big Head twisted his face up and held up the middle finger. Woo saw him through the mirror's reflection, still laughing.

Seeing their destination up ahead, Killa Dre pulled over alongside the curb and murdered the engine. He hopped out of the whip first, followed by Woo and Big Head. The threesome mobbed towards the black gate of a white two story house with a charcoal gray roof. As soon as they entered the yard they were greeted by a collective of four men who were shooting the shit until they arrived. These men ranged from their mid to late twenties and held affiliation to the infamous Eastside Outlaws Rolling Twenties Bloods.

There was Big Panic, a six foot two, three hundred pound man with a shaved meaty head and a thick beard. He was built like a refrigerator with hands the size of boxing gloves. He was no joke, and he made it his business to make sure no one ever thought so.

The six foot one mahogany complexioned dude beside him, stroking his nappy beard with an unmanicured hand was Gouch. This man was a stone cold killer with a fierce reputation. He was a mothafucking beast with his twin Berettas, which he nicknamed The Girls. Under no circumstances was he to be played with.

Gouch had been studying the Nin Jit Su style of fighting since he was six years old. Seeing him in front of the television set mimicking the martial arts moves he saw in Kung Fu flicks, his grandmother decided to enroll him into a dojo in downtown Los Angeles. The lanky killer got real nice with his hands. In fact, he had never lost a fight.

The brown skinned fellow posted at his left who wore his hair in six neat cornrows that curled like snakes at the middle of his back was the seasoned killer's younger brother, Pavielle, also known as O.G Booby Loco. He wasn't as trigger-happy as his brother, but he'd have a fool's momma buying a black dress in a New York minute. You didn't get to be an O.G before you turned twenty-three without busting a few heads. Like his uncle Gangsta before him, he was all about a dollar; he breathed to hustle. He often joked that all he needed in life was G.M.B: Guns, Money and Bitches.

"Where you get that shit from, Killa?" Pavielle asked of the L he'd just taken from him.

"That Rasta that be slanging them bootlegs out in front of Superior market."Killa Dre answered, throwing his hood on his head and sticking his hands inside of pockets.

"For real?"

"Yep."

"I just copped an ounce from 'em, but the shit fiya,"

he informed him. "Nigga said if I'm tryna fuck with something larger than that then he'd have to get with his people. I got his contact. I know yo' unc been looking for a better plug on the shit than he got, so I figured maybe they could work something out."

"Good looking out." Pavielle nodded, taking the card that his little homie passed him. "The shit we be getting from the eses ain't got shit on this." He admired the blunt that was pinched between his fingers, smoke rising from it and evaporating into the air. Pavielle kneeled down and stroked the black shiny coat of his Rottweiler.

"Yeah, we gone have to rush that, fa' sho'," Gouch nodded, blowing smoke from his nostrils after taking a couple of puffs of that shit.

"Y'all hogging the mothafucka all up and shit," Panic complained, having just taken the L from him.

"Relax, fat boy, it's enough for everybody." Gouch chuckled. "Killa said he gotta ounce, right?" he looked at the young head bussa.

Killa Dre spat on the ground and looked back up, nodding. He pulled an ounce from out of his pocket and passed it to Gouch. He smiled happily and held the Ziploc to his nose, taking a deep inhalation.

"How you been holding up, my nigga?" Pavielle asked him of his dealing with his brother's death.

"I'm solid, big homie. I would be doing a lot better if I could put the tool to the fool that smashed my big bro though." His eyes bled his truth. He knew that he could not rest until the nigga that had popped his sibling was six feet under.

Pavielle threw his arm around the little nigga'z shoulders and said, "We gone find this nigga. I promise you that. Mel was just as much my brother as he was yours." He spoke sincerely. Pavielle felt bad when he'd heard that Tramel had been claimed by the streets. He'd known him and Killa Dre all of their lives. Sometimes he'd give them rides home from school or play football in the streets with them and their friends. The Johnson Boys reminded him of himself and Gouch coming up, which was why he'd taken such a liking to them. Although Killa signed up for the troubles that the life brought, Tramel was headed down a completely different path. He had a bright future ahead of him, but that all came to a tragic end when he was shot down like a goddamn rabid dog in the streets.

"Fa sho'," Killa Dre gave him a complex handshake and pounded the Blood gang sign against his chest.

Hearing a man's soulful voice and a shopping cart being rolled brought everyone's attention to the black gate.

"New school, I got something for you." Avenue smiled as he moved his way into the yard pushing a shopping cart loaded with junk he'd collected throughout the day.

Woof! Woof! Woof! Woof!

Pavielle's Rottweiler went ham when it saw Avenue, struggling to get loose from its owner. He growled and barked viciously causing spittle to fly from its mouth. He leaped forward but Pavielle yanked back on the chain of his spiked collar, pulling him down. If it wasn't for the beast being on the leash he would have surely tried to rip the junky limb from limb.

"Damu, sit your ass down!" Pavielle smacked the dog on his ass and it calmed down, sitting on its hind legs.

Avenue was an older cat; about sixty years old. A tall dude with a slender frame, he rocked a shabby afro that looked like tangled barbed wire and unkempt facial hair. His smoked out ass used to be the lead singer of an R&B group called The Mesmerizers. The quartet was a group whose talents rivaled The Temptations. The singers were internationally known and were well acquainted with fame and fortune.

The sky was the limit for old Avenue. That was until he managed to get hooked on crack cocaine. In a couple of years he pissed away his publishing, his houses, his cars, and his jewelry. The crack guerilla came with a broom and swept away all of his assets, including his position in The Mesmerizers.

The D-boys christened him Avenue because he would break out in song and dance at any given moment on the avenue where they were slinging. High out of his mind, Avenue would imagine that he was back on stage with his old group performing one of their many hit songs. His performance would be so good that the hustlers would bless him with nickel and dime crack rocks.

"What chu got for me, old school?" Pavielle asked, switching hands with the chain that held Damu.

"Top secret, for your eyes only," Avenue said in a hushed tone, holding his hand to the side of his mouth.

"Alright," Pavielle said before chaining Damu up to a tree. He turned to Avenue, placing his hand to his back.

"Step into my office." He led him into a darkened area on the side of the house where they wouldn't be seen. "Now, what chu got that's especially for me?"

Avenue held up a finger before stepping around his shopping cart. He took a cautious look around before moving about some of the junk inside of the cart until he found what he was looking for. He pulled out something wrapped in a tattered blanket and sat it on the hood of Pavielle's Chevy Impala. He un-wrapped the blanket and revealed the AK-47 it was concealing. Pavielle's eyes grew big. He whistled when he saw the assault rifle. He stepped to it, gently sweeping his hand up and down the length of it.

"There you go, baby boy, ain't she a beaut?" Avenue asked, smiling from ear to ear, putting his beige, rotten teeth on display, "Brand spanking new, straight outta the box."

Pavielle picked up the AK-47 and slowly swept it back and forth, imagining cutting his enemies in half with it.

"Where'd you get this big mothafucka?"

"Never mind that, do you want her?"

"Hell yeah, I want her." Pavielle said, like '*Nigga, you don't even have to ask that*'. "How much you want for me to walk off with her?" he looked from the assault rifle to Avenue. He saw his mouth biting to the right. This meant that he was fucked up in the game and needed a blast of crack badly. There wasn't any telling when he had his last hit. Seeing this let Pavielle know that he could take the AK-47 off of the crackhead's hands for a little of nothing.

Avenue scratched his nappy facial hair as he thought on a price. Pavielle cringed as he imagined him as a dog with fleas.

"I'll tell you what, since I fuck with you hard body," he tapped his fist over his heart, "gone throw me four of dem dead white men and gone 'bout ya business."

"Three."

"Three? Come on now, new school, you tryna beat me like I stole something, man." He balled up his face.

"Nigga, you show up outta nowhere with a choppa, I know you done stole it." Pavielle angled his head and twisted his lips. He looked at him like *'Come on now. You know that I know better'.* "I'll drop you three, homie, for all I know this mothafucka gotta couple hot ones on it."

"G, I told you that bad boy clean. Trust me, folks."

"Nigga, I don't trust nobody," He spoke from the heart, "Either take the three or bounce with this mothafucka, and risk getting caught with it and catching ten."

"Mannnnn," Avenue blew hard and massaged his chin as he thought on it. "You know you robbing me without the ski-mask and gun, right?"

Pavielle looked away rolling his eyes and running a hand down his face. The nigga was tired of the back and forth spat with old head. "What's up, fam? You gone let me get this off you or what?"

The crackhead sighed and said, "Yeah, G, gone and run me that for I start to regret it."

Pavielle sat the AK-47 down on the hood of the car and reached inside of his pocket. He'd just pulled out a roll of dead presidents when Avenue held up a hand.

"Wait a minute, new school, what cha doing?"

"I'm 'bout ta break you off."

"Naw, you know how I get down, I need my prescription filled."

"Oh, alright," he stuffed the roll of dead presidents back inside of his red Dickie's pocket. "Gone and see my nigga Debo on the seven, tell him I sent chu. He'll hook you up."

"Sho' ya right. My man," He said excitedly. Next, he slapped hands with Pavielle and swung his shopping cart around. He bopped off pushing the shopping cart and singing a song he and his group performed back in the day.

"What chu got there, baby boy?" Gouch approached with Panic by his side.

Pavielle picked the AK-47 back up and swung it around, pointing it at Gouch and stopping him in his tracks. "A choppa."

"Whoa!" Gouch held up his hands in surrender.

"Be easy, nigga." Panic spoke of Pavielle's handling of the AK-47.

Pavielle chuckled and smiled before turning the weapon over to Gouch, who gripped it and aimed it at something across the way.

"How much this mothafucka run you?" Gouch asked, barely audible with a blunt hanging from his lips.

"Three yards," Pavielle answered.

"So that's what that smoker fool had for you." Panic said. "At three B-notes that was a steal."

"Real spit," Pavielle agreed.

The sudden burst of automatic gunfire ripping through the air caused Pavielle and Panic to duck. Their hands went to grab the bangers on their waistbands, but when they saw that it was Gouch letting off the AK-47 in the air they dropped their hands.

"This mothafucka chunky, Blood, on me," Gouch claimed. He used one hand to take a pull from his blunt and used the other to hold the AK-47. He ogled the lethal weapon with admiration.

"Let me see it, Gucci." Panic took the AK-47 into his large hands.

"Y'all alright out here?" a voice rang out from behind the threesome. Pavielle turned around and found a dark figure clutching what looked like a gun from its shape. "We're straight, unc, just playing with my new toy."

"I suggest you put cha lil' toy up, 'cause Binem gone be sliding through here any minute." Gangsta told him.

"When you handle that come up stairs I need to holla at chu."

"Alright," Pavielle said. He turned around to Panic who was about to let the AK-47 off in the air again. Before the chocolate giant could pull the trigger, he snatched the weapon free of his possession.

"Gimmie my shit, man," Pavielle wrapped the AK-47 back up in the blanket and bopped off to stash his new toy.

"Youz a stingy ass nigga, Blood," Panic watched his road dawg walk away. He waved him off and went to join the other homies along with Gouch so they could finish talking shit and getting high.

Chapter Two

Vayda stepped inside of the bathroom closing the door shut behind her. Standing before the medicine cabinet's mirror, she removed her bra and panties, allowing them to drop into a pile at her feet. With her hands firmly on her hips, she smiled as she looked herself over, admiring her curvy form. Now, don't get it fucked up, light skin did have her flaws and all just like any other woman, but still, her body was remarkable. Her melon like breasts sagged and she had a pudgy stomach and stretch marks on her thighs and butt, but that's what made her so sexy. A person could tell that she was a real woman and real women weren't perfect like those chicks that they had on the cover of magazines, all airbrush painted with accessories and shit. Nah, real women had flawed bodies just like Vayda, and that's what made them desirable. Hell, it wasn't like her man was complaining. He loved everything about her, including her body. So as long as boo was happy she was happy.

Vayda patted her stomach and rubbed it, thinking about the life that was growing inside of her. She hadn't told Pavielle that she was expecting because she didn't know how to break the news to him. For that matter, she didn't know how he would take it. He could totally flip out on her and try to convince her to get an abortion, or he could be just as excited as she was. Her heart told her that hubby was going to be joyous once she told him that he was going to be a father, so she figured that she'd break the news to him soon.

Vayda turned to walk away from her reflection when she saw something in the mirror that caused her face to ball up. She turned to the side and looked over her shoulder at her reflection. Along down her back she saw several keloid welts that overlapped each other. She didn't know how she could ever forget that they were there, but from time to time she managed to do just that. Tears built up in her eyes and obscured her vision making it seem as if she was looking through a crystal. Her pain came running down her face in buckets and she whimpered, quickly smacking her hands over her mouth. Her shoulders shuddered as she stared at herself in the mirror. She'd never forget the night that she'd gotten such ugly scars, or the man that had given them to her. She remembered them scrapping over her trap being short. Although she'd gotten in a few good punches, it was his blow to her jaw that left her on the receiving end of a possible loss.

***

Buddy scrambled to his feet, his jeweled hand clutching a straight razor. His hairy chest jumped up and down as he breathed heavily, cheeks huffing and puffing. His usually curly hair was a mess. There was a swelling under his right eye and his silk blue shirt was torn. He wiped his swollen bleeding lip with the back of his fist and swallowed the blood that had filled his grill. It tasted of metal but he didn't acknowledge it. Nah, his attention was solely focused on Vayda who was crawling away from him. Her eyes were set on her handbag which had her nickel plated .22 hanging halfway out of it.

"Fuck you think you goin' bitch? I ain't done witcho mothafuckin' ass yet, not by a long shot." he swore, his lethal eyes held firmly on her as he stalked after her, taking his sweet time. "I'ma carve you up like a Christmas goose." He licked his chops and bit down on his bottom lip.

Tears flooded Vayda's swollen face, mixing in with the blood running from her nose. She moved as fast as she could with a twisted ankle, trying to make it to her handbag where she knew her piece was. Buddy had given it to her in case some trick overstepped his boundaries and she had to set him straight. Now she had every intention of using it on his ass if she able to get her hands on it.

Vayda had just grabbed her handbag and gripped the small gun when she saw Buddy's shadow eclipse her on the carpet. Her eyes widened with fear and she gasped. His grunting flooded her ears and she felt fire rip back and forth across her back. Through the floor she saw his shadow swinging a straight razor back and forth across her back causing her to grimace, narrowing her eyelids into slits. She shrieked in excruciation and tried to reach over her shoulder instinctively to stop him, but he started slashing at her hand as well, opening up a nasty gash on it.

Vayda howled in pain and looked at her ruined hand, oozing with bright red blood. Her mind was quickly taken away from the pain though, because he continued to hack away at her rear, making it look like bleeding pastrami meat. "Arghhhhh!" Tears flushed down her cheeks and she bit down hard on her bottom lip to combat the excruciation from the blazing fire in her back. Gripping the small gun with both hands, she turned around on her back and pointed the deadly end of her weapon at her attacker's chest. He froze where he stood, with his head tilted down, chin resting in his chest. His eyebrows were lowered and he was glaring down at her, lips peeled back into a sneer. His shoulders rose and fell as he breathed, blood droplets falling from the end of his blade, soiling the carpet.

"Now, just what in the fuck do you plan on doing with that, huh? Yo' lil' red ass ain't built for no mur…" Pow! A shot to his chest cut his shit talking short. His eyes widen with surprise and his mouth hung open. He touched the hole *in his chest and his palm came away crimson. He couldn't believe it. That bitch had really shot him. "You...you...you fuckin' whore!" he roared and his eyes darkened with hatred. Screaming in a rage, he charged at her with his razor held above his head ready to slice her down to the bone. Squeezing her eyelids shut tightly, Vayda pulled back on the trigger of her weapon. It kicked back when it spat back to back, propelling him backwards with every bullet released. Pow! Pow! Pow! Pow! Buddy dropped his straight razor as he went staggering back, getting tangled up in the curtains and crashing through the window's glass. He hollered out as he went hurtling towards the apartment complex's parking lot. Still clutching her gun and wincing, Vayda slowly scrambled to her feet, clenching her jaws to combat the sharp pains zipping back and forth across her back. She crept towards the window with precaution and placed her back up against the side of it. Carefully, she looked over and out of the window. A surprised expression went across her face when she only saw broken glass and the curtains below. Figuring that she'd better get the hell out of there before he or the police came looking for her, she packed a bag and stole the money Buddy had stashed inside of the speaker box in his bedroom. That night she hopped on a Greyhound to Los Angeles where she found a job as a cashier at Louisiana fried chicken and met Pavielle shortly thereafter.*

Vayda wiped her eyes and face with her hands and then looked back up at her reflection smiling. The nightmare that she had experienced back then was over and now she was living a dream come true with the man that she deserved. Meeting Pavielle had been the best thing that had happened to her. She was sure that once she told him about the baby that he would be just as happy as she was. Having been in and out of foster homes all of her life, Vayda didn't know what it was like to have a family and a stable place to call home. So she couldn't wait for the day to come for her to have one all of her own. Something told her that this was it. This was the time to finally settle down and get the one thing she'd been missing all of her life…a family.

After plugging up the curling iron so it could get hot so she could do her hair once she'd gotten out of the shower, she turned on the dials that operated the shower. Hot water came spraying out of the showerhead, quickly filling the bathroom with a fog that masked the medicine cabinet's mirror. She pulled her curly hair back up in a ponytail at the top of her head and tangled a rubber band around it so that her hair wouldn't get wet. Afterwards, she stepped inside of the tub and grabbed a loofer, soaping it up with Dove body wash. She smiled and sung as she lathered her form, masking herself with white foam from her neck on down.

***

Pavielle knocked on his uncle's bedroom door.

"Come in." Gangsta called out from the other side of the door. As soon as Pavielle crossed the threshold into his uncle's bedroom he was struck by his attire. Gangsta was razor sharp. He was G'd up in a feathered brim, cream tailored suit, tie, baby blue button-down and two tone snakeskin Stacy Adams.

Gangsta was a ruggedly handsome man with a caramel hue. He wore his hair in a fade that blended in perfectly with his thin goatee. He was six feet tall and had the physique of Lou Ferrigno. He had diamond earrings in both ears. His eyes were hidden behind gold frames and a Presidential Rolex hugged his wrist. On his pinky finger there was an icy ring worthy of a mafia don.

"Damn, unc, don't hurt'em!" Pavielle said, plopping down on the king sized bed.

"This is that O.G shit. What chu know about it, young nigga?" Gangsta asked as he adjusted his cufflinks and struck poses fit to bless the cover of GQ Magazine.

"Whoo! Is that O.G Gangsta from The Bottoms that's killing them fools in that tailored and them Stacy's? Get'em, unc."Pavielle smiled amusingly, looking on at his uncle.

"Shiiieet, I'm fresh to death, niggaz can't tell me nothing." he adjusted his tie in the mirror.

"Aye, unc, what was it you wanted to see me about?" wonderment crossed his face.

"Got a couple pounds of Kush I want chu to break down and bag up into twenty-five dollar sacks."

Gangsta's father died of a heart attack when he was seventeen years old, leaving him the man of the house. Seeing his mother struggling to keep a roof over their heads and food on the table, he took it to the streets to "Get It How He Lived". He started off selling drugs hand over fist but eventually graduated to being the neighborhood's dope man. From there he had his section of The Low Bottoms on lock. A nigga couldn't get money by his way if he wasn't copping from him or kicking up money for taxes. That's just how it was. His word was law and if anybody went against the grain they faced certain death. Straight like that.

Pavielle and Gouch's parents were murdered when they were little, leaving Gangsta the only male in the boys lives. The O.G knew his nephews praised him as if he was a holy figure, and therefore they would hold onto his words as if they were gospel. So he took it upon himself to administer some kind of guidance. He was helping his mother raise his nephews as best as he could. He loved the brothers as if they were his sons. He knew the dangers of his lifestyle and how alluring it could be to his nephews. He found himself playing tug-of-war with their lives, with him pulling them in one direction and the streets pulling them in the other. It was a battle he ended up losing.

"Where is it?"

"Under the bed there."

Pavielle reached under the bed and pulled out a duffle bag. He sat it on his lap and unzipped it. He pulled out two pounds of Purple Kush in Ziploc bags. The weed was so potent that he could smell it through the Ziplocs. He knew that this was that fire. Pavielle unzipped the Ziploc bags and inhaled the odor of the rich green buds sprinkled with purple crystals that were inside. He flinched as the strong aroma came into his contact with his nasal passages.

"Damn, unc, this is that Oooh wee!" Pavielle declared closing the Ziploc and shoving it back into the duffle bag. "So, where are you headed? You gotta hot date tonight?"

"It's that time of the month again; I gotta go see my boy." Gangsta said. That "*Boy*" he was referring to was his cocaine connection, Jesus Arturo, known in the streets as

Black Jesus. He was meeting the Mexican kingpin at a Spanish restaurant where they were to make a drop off and exchange.

"So who are you taking, Shafonda?" Pavielle inquired.

"Nah, she can't make it so I'm taking Vayda." Gangsta told him, fixing his brim on his head.

Pavielle's face gave to a scowl hearing that the woman his uncle was taking out was his own.

"Who?" he frowned, trying to make sure he had heard right.

"Who did you say?"

"You heard right. Vayda…your girl," Gangsta said again. "Shafonda cancelled on me at the last minute; something about her mother being sick or some shit. But

I'm not complaining. Shafonda's fine, but she don't have shit on Vayda." He tucked the chrome, pearl handle .45 automatic into the small of his back.

Pavielle flashed his uncle a slight grin to hide his jealousy, but the O.G could tell that taking his lady out didn't sit too well with him. He knew firsthand how jealous his nephew could get; plenty of men had lost their lives trying to get next to Vayda.

"Vayda saved my life." Gangsta confessed. "I offered to lay a few dollars on her…"

"But I wasn't having it!" a female voice said from the doorway.

Pavielle and Gangsta whip their heads around to the door way; their eyes doubled in size and their mouths dropped open in awe, seeing the gorgeous redbone before them. Vayda's curvaceous body filled out a strapless white Dolce & Gabana dress. Her small manicured feet were in a pair of pink Steve Madden high heels. Her hair was pulled back in a bun to show off her pink diamond earrings Pavielle bought her for her twenty-second birthday. A platinum & pink diamond necklace adorned her neck and a Jaeger Lecoultre watch with pink diamonds surrounding its face graced her wrist. The dress and all of the accessories complimented Vayda's beauty well. She looked like she was ready to attend The Ball with Cinderella.

Gangsta whistled as he took in the sight that was the gorgeous Ms. Vayda Perry. He looked over to Pavielle who still had his mouth open, saliva had pooled in his mouth and drool threatened to drip from the corner of it. Vayda was even more beautiful than the day he first met her.

***

"Man, I'm hungrier than a hostage!" Panic claimed, pushing his blood red, big body Suburban on those chrome thangs through the streets.

"Shit, what chu tryna grab to eat?" Pavielle asked.

"I don't know. I could go for some Cantonese food; you tryna fuck with Paul's Kitchen."

"I've gotta taste for some chicken and fries." Pavielle said.

"What about some Church's?"

"Blood, you the only nigga I know that like that nasty ass Church's Chicken!" Panic said, shaking his head. "I don't really have a taste for no bird, but I'll tell you what, though. There's a Louisiana Fried Chicken spot on the corner of Manchester and Normandie. They have chicken and Chinese food there."

"Bool, but ain't that Eight Trey hood?"

"Yeah, but we're good, though. I know a couple of Treys," Panic told him. "Some of my family is from their set."

"I Griff you, but that ain't enough insurance for me."

Panic reached over him, popped open the glove-box, and produced a Glock .9mm. He tossed the compact gun onto his lap and smacked the glove-box back shut.

"There! Is that enough insurance for you?" the big man grinned.

"Nah," Pavielle examined the Glock in his lap. "But this is..." he brandished a banger of his own. It was a Desert Eagle, easily twice the size of Panic's weapon.

They both laughed.

***

When Panic and Pavielle hopped out of the Suburban and approached the chicken spot they noticed there were mostly old people and females inside, which was fine by Pavielle because he wasn't looking for trouble. He just wanted to grab a bite to eat. The entire way over to the chicken spot his stomach was talking to him like that plant in The Little Shop of Horrors movie. Feed me, Booby! Feed me!

Pavielle and Panic pushed their way through the double doors of the hood establishment. As soon as Pavielle stepped to the window to place his order, he was hypnotized and at a loss for words for the beauty behind the cash register. Little momma was finer than a mothafucka, and she was working the hell out that red and black uniform. Redbone was banging like a B.G that had just finished getting processed through the county jail. She possessed a face and a body that deserved the cover of Smooth Magazine. She had a rose gold complexion and smooth blotch less skin. Her long curly, sandy brown hair fell just past her shoulders. And her eyes were a greenish blue, depending on where she was standing when the light hit her.

Vayda snapped her fingers before Pavielle's eyes trying to snap him out of his daze.

"Hi there," She smiled after snapping Pavielle out of his daze. "May I take your order, please?"

"Blood, what the fuck is wrong with you?" Panic frowned, looking from his nigga to the cashier. "Order your mothafucking food so we can bounce."

"Oh, sorry about that," Pavielle apologized.

"It's okay." Vayda giggled. "Our low prices tend to do that to the customers. They're stunned by how good and affordable the grub is here."

"Oh, it ain't the grub here that's got me tripping," Pavielle confessed. "Believe that."

Vayda blushed and smiled, she couldn't help herself; the young nigga was just how she liked her men, cute and thuggish.

"Oh, she smiles?" Pavielle eyed the redbone seductively. Vayda shook her head and took on a more serious approach.

"May I take your order, sir?" She asked. Catching on, Pavielle straightened himself out

"Alright," he looked over the menu above her head.

"Let me get a two piece; a breast and a wing, a small fries, a large lemonade, no ice, a sweet potato pie and, uh, your name and your phone number." He said slyly, pulling out a wad of $100 dollar bills from his pocket. He made sure the crisp roll of Benjamin Franklins were before the redbone's eyes. He wanted her to know that he was holding, and that he wasn't just some bum ass nigga trying to spit game.

"Sorry, sweetie, but my name and number aren't on the menu." Vayda stated seriously, the least bit impressed by his money. She punched in the total of his meal on the register. "Eight twenty-five is your total, sir." She said with a no none sense attitude.

Pavielle peeled of a $100 dollar bill and handed it to her. She handed him back his change and left to prepare his food; as soon as she was out of earshot Panic started in on Pavielle.

"Ah, Blood!" Panic laughed. "Light skin dissed you, kid."

"Shut up, fat boy!" Pavielle said, playfully throwing jabs and punches at the refrigerator of a man. Once Pavielle and Panic were back in the Suburban they checked their food to make sure everything was there. The first thing the young nigga noticed when cracking open his chicken

box was the cashier's name and telephone number scribbled on the receipt. Right below the ten digits was a purple lip-stick print kiss. The same color of the lip-stick that the curly haired beauty had on. Pavielle picked up the receipt and stashed it in his pocket. He smiled and boasted the redbone's digits in Panic's face.

Pavielle called Vayda the next night and they had an in depth conversation that lasted three hours. He found out some interesting things about Vayda. For instance, she was Creole, left handed and spoke three different languages: Spanish, French and German. She was quite the artist and had moved from Oakland to Los Angeles not too long ago. She filled him in on being shuffled through the foster care system, living from pillar to post, and her relationship with Buddy. She gave him the rundown and didn't leave anything out. The way she figured he was going to accept her or he was going to move the fuck on. She'd rather put everything out in the open.

After their conversation they made plans to go out the next night. Instead of the traditional dinner and a movie outing, Pavielle decided to switch things up and take Vayda to an African American Heritage Museum at the coliseum. Afterwards, they went go-kart racing, played the arcade and ate at a restaurant called the Fish and Grill in Gardena. At the end of the night, Pavielle laid a blanket on the roof of his '96 Chevy Impala SS and they spent the remainder of the night staring up at the moon and scattered stars, talking. From that day forth the pair was inseparable.

***

"Damn, I must really look good." Vayda said, approaching Pavielle and closing his bottom jaw to his top one.

"Oh, you're all of that and a bag of uncut dope." Gangsta took her hand and kissed it.

"Why thank you, Gangsta," Vayda blushed and took him in, "You don't clean up too bad yourself."

"Are you ready to go?"

"I'm ready when you are."

With that said, Pavielle snapped out of his daze and rose to his feet.

Gangsta embraced his youngest nephew as if he was on his way to prison and was saying his last goodbye.

"Don't worry, nephew," He whispered into his ear. "I won't fuck her. At least not tonight I won't." He pecked Pavielle on the cheek and laughed, smacking him on the back. Seeing that he wasn't feeling his sense of humor took the jovial expression off of his face. "Ah, I'm fucking with you, nigga. Redbone is in good hands," He assured him before hooking his arm with Vayda's. "I'll take care of her."

"I'ma hold you to that, old nigga." Pavielle said seriously.

"Shall we?" Gangsta asked Vayda.

"Yes, we shall." She replied.

After closing the door behind Gangsta and Vayda, Pavielle grabbed everything he needed to break down both pounds of Kush. He took the digital scale from the top dresser drawer along with the sandwich bags. He then got the food-tray stand from out of the closet and set it up beside the bed. Sitting behind the food-tray stand, he dumped the contents of the first Ziploc of Kush onto the tray and proceeded to break it down.

Working for their uncle, Pavielle and Gouch hustled everything from hash to crack cocaine. Gangsta showed them the ropes when they were coming up so they knew how to cook, cut, and rock the product up. While Gouch could hustle he wasn't as good as his baby brother. Pavielle could tell how much the product was worth just from looking at it. He was what you would call a natural born hustler. Back in grade school he would sell the kids candy, bubblegum, potato chips, sodas and cookies and by the end of the day he'd leave with one hundred and fifty dollars profit. He'd sneak Gangsta's old dirty magazines from home and charge his friends at school a dollar a peek. And when Wrestle Mania came around, he'd charge the neighborhood kids two dollars a head to watch it on the big screen television in his grandmother's den. The hustle was definitely in the young nigga'z blood, some would even argue that he was even better at it than Gangsta.

Working for his uncle was cool and the money was straight, but he couldn't see himself under his uncle's wing for the rest of his life, he had bigger aspirations. He wanted to be the man someday, too. He wanted to be more than just the neighborhood dope man; he wanted to hold the title of kingpin.

Chapter Three

A young man sat duct-taped to an iron chair inside of a dark basement. The chain linked light bulb dangling from above, illuminated a light that exposed the damages of the brutal beating he'd taken. He had a golf ball size knot on his forehead, an eye that was swollen shut and a broken nose that had doubled in size. His face was bruised black and blue. A series of tiny cuts littered his face, and their bleeding had run down his neck and stained the chest of his wife beater pink. He looked around at his four captors with trembling legs, piss dripping from the edge of his chair and making a small puddle at his feet.

"Sun, I suggest you tell us where our money is before level two of this interrogation begins, and believe me, if you've seen what these eyes have seen Supa do to cats with his torture methods...Let's not take it that far. Let's end this now. What did you do with the money you stole?" Casanova asked him, sounding calm and sincere. He was damn near convincing. Casanova, or Double O.G Cas, as he was called was the oldest homie present at sixty-two. He had a thick crop of salt & pepper dreadlocks that hung over his shoulders and back and a matching beard. His neck was thick and his body was rippled with muscles. Casanova was a member of the Eastside Crips as well as the Five Percenters.

The young man looked to Supacrip who was removing the bloody brass-knuckles that he'd just finished using on him. He had put on some goggles and was pulling on yellow dishwashing gloves. Only God knew what he had in store for the youth. He wore an evil smile as he tried to decide what power tool to use on his capture.

"Man, this nigga ain't gone talk, Cuz." Nike said, looking at the number Supacrip had done on the young man duct-taped to the chair. Nike was a short, muscular cat that wore his hair short and wavy. He'd gotten his name from the Nike logo scar under his right-eye. Killing was his hobby and slinging crack was his habit. He was slowly churning out a resume that was as lengthy and brutal as some of the notorious gangsters his hood had the misfortune of producing.

"Nah, this bitch ass nigga gone tell me where my money is," C-note exclaimed with a Belizean accent. He was a caramel complexion brother with a crown of naturally curly hair he wore in a taper-fade. He screwed the cap off a bottle of rubbing alcohol and splashed it on the capture's wounds. The young man whipped his head back and forth, screaming in agony and thrashing around in the chair. "Shit feels like acid when it hits them open wounds and shit, don't it? Well, it's gone get a hell of a lot worse before we're done." He harped up spit and spat on the young man before throwing the bottle at his head.

"Fuck is your cousin, Nike?" He whipped around to the shorter man yelling with clenched fists.

Nike shrugged. "Cuz, said he was on his way like fifteen minutes ago." He glanced at his watch and pulled out his cell. "I'ma 'bout to call him again," He began punching a number on the digital screen of his cell.

"No need, I'm already here," Nightmare said as he descended the staircase with a pit bull on a chain leading the way. He was a tall dark skinned dude with a face that belonged on the F.B.I's most wanted poster. His rap sheet boasted everything from robbery to attempted murder. He had a blue bandana tied around his head Aunty Jemima style and a blue button-down shirt with a bandana print.

Nightmare slapped hands with his homies before turning around to the young man. "Soooooo, this is the lil' nigga that cleaned us outta mill, huh?"

"Yep, that's him. He ain't talking but he will be in a sec," Supacrip opened and closed the hedge clippers rapidly, making the sharp metal blades cling. He threatening eyes bored into those of his victim's, sending volts of fear throughout his body. "One of y'all niggaz unzip his pants and pull out his dick."

"Ah, nah, Cuz, y'all gone cut off my shit?" The young man's head darted around at the faces surrounding him. "Please, man, don't cut off my dick. Oh, God! Help! Help!"

"Shut cho ho ass up," Nike pointed his pistol at the youth's head, putting him on mute and causing him to whimper.

"I'm not touching his dick," C-note frowned.

"I'm not doing it either." Cas said.

Supacrip looked to Nike. "Cuz, I don't know why you're looking this way."

"I'm doing all the torturing and shit. The least y'all could do is pull the nigga'z wang out." Supacrip reasoned.

"That's right; you're doing all of the torturing so you pull his thang out. This is your part of the game, sun." Cas told him.

"Fuck it, I'll do it. Hold these," Supacrip passed the hedge clippers to Nike. He started over in the young man's direction but Nightmare stopped him.

"Chill, no need to get that bloody, I'll find out where the nigga stashed our shit." Nightmare chained his pit to a pillar in the basement and approached the young man. He looked to be relieved that he wasn't about to have his penis severed.

"Nightmare, thank God you're here, Cuz. They..." the young man's words died in his throat as Nightmare brought his palm back and forth across his face.

Smack!

Smack!

Nightmare viciously smacked the youth across the face until he drew blood. He then wiped his hand off on the

young man's stained wife beater.

"Where the fuck is the money, nigga? I'm not gonna ask your ass again." Nightmare swore. Seeing its master agitated caused the pit bull to go wild barking and struggling to get off the chain.

"Nightmare, why are you doing me like this, fam? You know..." again he was put to silence by Nightmare vicious backhand slaps. The O.G crip's open palm felt like punches from all of his years of pumping iron. The blows had left the youth dazed and barely conscious. Nightmare leaned in close to him so no one could hear him. "Did y'all put the loot up where I told you to?" the young man mumbled some jargon he couldn't understand. Nightmare grabbed him by his jaw and looked him in the eyes, a mixture of blood and saliva oozed down his hand. "Come on now. I'm tryna get chu outta here, but chu gotta let me know where you stashed that paper. Did it make it to the spot where we agreed to meet?"

"Yeah... yeah, man. We stashed it under the

floorboards inside of the living...room."

"Alright, good," Nightmare gently patted him on the cheek and turned around to his comrades, pulling a chrome Desert Eagle from his waistband.

Blam!

"Ahhh," Irv yelled out in agony as a bullet tore through his small intestine and dropped him to the basement floor.

He'd been lurking in the shadows of the basement the whole time. He was so quiet that everyone had forgotten that he was there except the young man duct taped to the chair. He'd been snarling and giving him the evil eye warning him not to say anything about the money

they'd stole from one of the stash houses.

"Fuck you shoot Irv for, Cuz?" Nike's face balled up.

"He was with Dizzy when he robbed us, said it was all his idea." Nightmare informed him. "Where's our money, Irv?"

"You know where the fuck it's at, don't play stupid." He spat blood on the ground.

Nightmare blew a hole through Irv's hand and he hollered out in excruciation, cradling his mitt. "You got some more smart shit to say, tough guy?"

"Yeah, suck my dick, bitch!" Irv roared back

defiantly. That was the last words he'd ever speak. A bullet through the skull guaranteed that. Irv hit the floor bug eyed, leaving a splatter that was a combination of blood and brain matter scattered over the floor.

Nightmare pulled a gold Desert Eagle from his waistband and turned around to the young man duct-taped to the chair. Seeing the gleam of something shiny and gold caused the youth to snap out of his daze. He was about to plead his case when a bullet sent him to a place where it's always hot.

"What the fuck, man!" C-note bellowed. "How are we going to find our money now?"

"That's what I wanna know." Cas added, you could tell he was pissed but he was trying to hide it. He was normally a man who kept a cool and calm head.

"Dizzy told me they used the loot to pay a debt to some

Haitians before I slept him." Nightmare lied. "I just asked

Irv to see if he'd lied."

"You couldn't have left one of them alive to tell us where to find these cock suckas, man?" C-Note asked.

"What chu plan on doing? Putting the love on the dreads, fam?" Cas inquired.

"You damn right, don't nobody take nothing of mine, 'cause if they do they'll have the devil on their heels."

"Think, young brotha," Cas pointed a finger to his temple. "A war is only gone cost us more paper...maybe more than we've already lost."

"We're not about to take another loss, fuck that!" C-note said.

"We're not," Nightmare said to C-note. "But you are."

"Fuck you figure, nigga?"

"Before we started this union we all agreed that we'd be responsible for whoever we brought into the fold. If my memory serves me correct, it was you that brought Dizzy and Irv on."

"True." Cas nodded.

"Them are your boys, fam." Nike added.

C-Note looked around at all of the faces in the basement; everyone seemed to agree. "Alright, fuck it, y'all got that. I'll have Crow bring y'all that paper tomorrow evening." C-Note hated to take the blame but it was true they all agreed on that very ruling. "That ain't nothing but a lil' short paper anyway."

"Spoken like a true boss." Cas smiled and patted his shoulder.

"Cool," Nightmare tucked his Desert Eagles in his waistband. "Nike, Supa, y'all get rid of these bodies. I got some place I gotta be."

***

Nightmare pressed his ear against the dusty wood floorboards and listened for an area that wasn't shallow as he knocked around on it with a crowbar. Finding an area that wasn't shallow he smiled wickedly and drove the crowbar into the slight openings between the boards. One by one he popped the boards up and removed them until he revealed a dingy beige sack beneath them. He opened up the sack and found it loaded with wrinkled rubber-band stacks of cash. He smiled like The Grinch that stole Christmas.

Nightmare was one of the sleaziest and cleverest sons of bitch's to have ever breathed air. He'd gotten Irv and Dizzy to rob the spot where the money was collected at the end of the month from crack sales with promises that they could split $500 grand two ways while he kept the other five for himself. The deal sounded too sweet for the knuckleheads to pass up so they went through with it not knowing they were dealing with the devil reincarnated. Nightmare had always planned to walk off with the money, only he was going to off the twosome back at the condemned house. When Nike ran back the surveillance footage in the spot he found that it was Dizzy that robbed them. It threw a wrench in Nightmare's plan but he still managed to turn the table in his favor.

"You find it, daddy?" Bobby Blue turned around from where she was peering through the boarded up window, gripping a Russian Ruger.

"Yeah, take this to the car," Nightmare sat the sack aside.

Bobby Blue's leopard print red bottom Christian Louboutin's echoed on the wood floorboards as she approached Nightmare, blowing pink bubbles out of her

Bubble Yum. She was in a leopard print spandex shirt and matching skirt that hugged her body.

Bobby Blue was Nightmare's ride or die chick; his numbre uno. She had been with him since she was fourteen and he was eighteen. While other chicks had come and gone old Bobby Blue was still around holding the gangster crip down.

She was quite the vision with her long, wavy hair, smooth coco skin and light brown eyes, all of which were compliments of her Ethiopian heritage. The dimples in her cheeks and chin were the perfect marriage to her baby face. Her balloon breasts and shapely round ass was all natural. Though most swore she had some work done. Standing at five ten, she was one Amazon of a woman.

Bobby's father named her after the lead singer in the jazz band he played with back home. Ms. Bobby Latoya Blue died of a heroin over dose. Her band mates found her in the back bathroom of the club they were performing at that night dead. She was slumped upon the commode with a syringe needle in her arm and a tourniquet tied above her forearm.

While Nightmare began putting the floorboards back in place, Bobby picked up the sack and carried it out towards the backdoor. Most men would have been leery about having their woman go off with so much money, but

Nightmare had complete faith in his game. He'd trained Bobby well and knew she'd be loyal to him without a fault.

Present

Nightmare lay in bed taking pulls of a blunt with Bobby asleep beside him. The lights were out and the blue glow of the flat-screen was reflecting on his face. *The*

Honey Mooners were on but he wasn't paying the show any mind; his conversation over the telephone had his sole attention.

"Nothing, ma, I been good." he blew smoke up into the air and licked his lips. "Oh yeah, where's Shantell and Lil' Tay? That boy getting big than a mug, he's gone be taller than me in a minute. Who? Oh, Bobby," he glanced at her and she grunted and smacked her lips, rearranging herself in bed. "She's knocked out. I'll tell her you said hey. I'll slide through there later on tomorrow. Okilla, cool, I love you, too." He disconnected the call and sat the cell phone down on the nightstand. Having wrapped up the phone call, Nightmare went to light the end of his blunt again and found that the lighter wouldn't strike a flame. He shook it up and tried it once more but it still didn't work. Pulling open the top dresser drawer, he fished around inside of it until he found another lighter. He'd just pulled it out when he saw something that caused his forehead to indent. Sitting the lighter aside on the dresser, he picked up an old photo of him and his father.

The man known as David Grant Sr. looked to be about twenty-one years old and holding a four year old Nightmare by his hand while standing beside an old Cadillac Deville. The gangsta crip cracked a grin reminiscing as he took casual pulls from the roach end of his L, eyelids narrowing. His thoughts drifted off to his father and the day that he had lost him. He'd been murdered in cold blood right in front of his eyes and he'd never forget how it all went down in a million years.

Nightmare thought back to the time he was expelled from school for bringing a knife. The only reason why he hadn't been caught with a gun was because his homeboy Knockout had gotten picked up with it the day before. To make a long story short, some kid snitched when they saw him practicing, drawing his knife in the boy's rest room. Before his ass could grace the seat at his desk in his home room class, the school police were hauling his black ass off. His old man had to leave work early to pick him up. Needless to say old David was hot as a firecracker.

Flashback

"I can't believe yo' ass, man, as hard as I work to make sure you and yo' sista are taken care of. Plus, have all of the lil' extra bullshit that ya'll want. Sssssss," Dave shook his head pitifully at his son, cutting his eyes at him. He was frowning and sneering, wanting so badly to sock his ass dead in his chest for having him have to leave work to pick his monkey ass up from school, "What the fuck you needa knife fa, DJ?"

"You know what I'm into, pop. I gotta stay strapped at all times." Young Nightmare told his old man what's up. "I can't be out here like a sitting duck. My enemies will pick me off out here."

"Enemies?" his face balled up and he bit down on his bottom lip hard. He balled his hand into a fist, looking back and forth between the windshield and his offspring, waiting his chance to fire on his ass. "What. The. Fuck. I. Tell. You. 'Bout. Dat. Gangbanging shit, huh? Huh?" he punched him harder and harder with each word that sprung from his lips, making him duck down with his arms covering his head to shield him. "You ain't gone be no mothafucking punk ass gangbanga, ya hear me?" he snatched the blue bandana from his back pocket and held down the button on the door panel that descended the window. He tossed the bandana out of the window and rolled the window back up. "I love you too much, son. You hear me?" he looked from his boy to the windshield, trying not to cause an accident. "I

love you too much to lose you to these streets." David grasped the steering wheel with both hands and breathed huskily, chest rising and falling rapidly. His eyes watered feeling like he had failed his son, because the streets held more sway over him than he did. Feeling wetness run down his face, he thought it was raining until he touched his cheek. That's when he knew that there were actually tears running down his face. Young Nightmare felt like shit seeing his father cry and knowing that he was the cause of it. His old man really was good to him. He worked twelve hour days, sometimes sixteen hours to take care of home. A lot of times he didn't get to see him, but when he was home he was always spending time with him and his sister, occasionally dropping jewels on them. As much as a pain in the ass that he was, the little nigga really did look up to his old man.

"I'm sorry, pop, I'ma straighten up and fly right, okay?" He said, opening the glove-box and removing a couple of McDonald napkins, passing them to his old man. He watched as he dabbed the wetness from his face away and balled up the napkin.

"Promise," He glanced at his son.

"Promise what?"

"That cho lil' ass is gone do right by me." David told him. "That you gone go to school, get good grades and take ya ass to a university. Hell, I'll even take community college. Any place where you can expand yo' education, and hopefully one day make a decent living. 'Cause I'll tell you, Junior, the white man's working ya old man like a slave just to get this lil' bit of money I'm getting."

"Okay, pop, I promise you."

"I'll remind you that a man keeps his word now." He lifted an eyebrow and pointed to him without taking his eyes

off the windshield. "I taught chu that. If you can't keep yo' word then you ain't shit."

"I know, pop, and I'ma keep mine...on the set." The youngster swore. This earned him a dirty look from his father. "I mean, I put that on me."

"Good boy." He pulled him closer and kissed him on top of his head, keeping his eyes on the windshield. "I love you, son."

"I love you too, pop," The youngling smiled, happy to be back in his father's good graces.

Dave took the time to slip a cigarette into his mouth and fired it up, puffing out smoke. "You wanna hit up the arcade and see a movie?"

"Hell...I mean, yeah, let's do it." He said excitedly.

Dave took the square from his lips and released smoke, fanning it with his hand. "We rolling then."

Night fell on the city leaving the street lights and car headlights to keep Los Angeles lit. Young Nightmare and his father came strolling out of Magic Johnson movie theater. His old man had his arm over his shoulders and was sucking on the straw of his fountain drink while his son finished off his hotdog. Once the youngster was done with the dog, he wiped his hands off with a napkin and tossed it aside. After his father apprehended his vehicle, they pulled out of the parking lot. They were driving through the streets talking about the movie they'd just seen when the flashing lights went off behind them. The red and blue lights spun around in circles, flashing through the inside of their car.

"Damn," Dave pounded the steering wheel with his fist, hating to have been stopped. Veins rolled up his neck and forehead. He was hotter than an African summer. This would make the fourth time that he was stopped today. He was sure that the police were only pulling him over on the

account of him driving an E-class Mercedes Benz. He was sick and tired of them fucking with him.

"What's up, pop?" Young Nightmare's head snapped back and forth between his father and over his shoulder at the police cruiser. His old man ignored him and pulled over to the side of the street, unbuckling his safety belt. "Pop, what's going on?"

"I'm tired of this shit, stay here, Junior."

Dave picked up his cell phone and speed dialed his lawyer before throwing open the driver side door. He hopped out and turned to face the officers.

"I'm getting tired of y'all fuckin' with me now," he hollered out to them, gripping his silver cellular phone. "I just called my lawyer and he's..." The headlights of the police cruiser deflected off of the cell phone causing it to gleam and appear as chrome gun to the police.

"He's gotta gun!" One officer blurted out and they both drew their weapons. Bop! Bop! Bop! Bop! Young Nightmare watched in horror as his father was filled with holes and the driver side window exploded from a rush of bullets. His eyes were wide open and his mouth was the shape of an O. Dave slid down to the ground still holding his cell with his head at a funny angle. His eyes had a spaced out look to them and his mouth was ajar. He had expired.

"Pop!" Young Nightmare screamed seeing his old man lifeless and bleeding, sitting in broken glass. Tears were running down his face as he was crawling over the driver seat and stepping out into the streets. He got down on his knees before his father and hugged his waist, ignoring the police's orders for him to get out of the way.

With his face pressed against his old man's chest, he whimpered and slobbered, muffling some of his cries.

Present

After his father's death, Nightmare was off the mothafucking chain. He got into everything that there was to get into that was illegal. He jumped off the porch early as hell and made his bones whacking niggaz for profit; anything to put food on the table. My nigga even tried his hand at pimping. If it was a dollar that could be made off it then he was with it. It didn't matter what the fuck it was. That's just how he was on it.

Nightmare came from a house hold that had both parents. His father worked in a warehouse and his mother was a certified nurse's assistant; most of the time neither of them was at home which left him and his sister to do whatever they pleased. While his kid sister, Shantell, was hanging out with the older chicks on the block he was kicking it with the local criminals picking up game and earning his place among them. It took some time but he eventually earned the label of a thorough young nigga that wasn't to be fucked with. And this was when the little bastard was only twelve years old.

Chapter Four

A Bentley Continental pulled up to the curb outside of the Spanish restaurant, *Chico's*. Gangsta exited his vehicle, walked around to the passenger side, and opened the door up for Vayda. After helping her from the car, Gangsta closed the door behind her and they made a beeline for the entrance of the restaurant. As soon as Gangsta and Vayda pushed their way through the double doors of the Spanish restaurant they were greeted by the loud music of the El Mariachi band playing on the stage. Standing at the door, Gangsta and Vayda took in the scenery. The Spanish restaurant was elegant and classy.

Black Jesus was in his wheelchair on the shiny, black marble dance floor dancing *The Salsa* with a fine Spanish mami in a red dress with a rose behind her ear. She had bronze skin, big brown eyes, and long silky hair that reached her ass. With his crown full of dark raven curls, Black Jesus was quite handsome. The Latin drug lord was an attractive man; a pretty boy some would argue. Though he was Mexican, he had skin the color of a Hershey's Kiss. In fact, when first laying eyes on him, you would think he was the descendent of African Americans until he'd opened his mouth and address you with that deep South American accent.

Before he was the drug lord that he was today, young Jesus Arturo was an active gangbanger running around reckless in the streets of South Central, Los Angeles. Back then thirteen year old Jesus was known for carrying twin black revolvers, both of which helped him garner the reputation of a killer; between him and his little brother, Bullet, the two had accumulated enough bodies under their belts to fill a cemetery. But that was a long time ago; the drug lord had put his guns away and picked up the hat of a business mogul. He was now over seeing a multimillion dollar drug empire.

Bullet sat with his back to the bar peeling an apple with a switchblade. He was so busy watching his brother out on the dance floor that he didn't notice Gangsta and Vayda had walked in. Although the youngest Auturo brother was Mexican his skin held the complexion of a white man. He had hazel green eyes and a trimmed mustache. The back of his shaved head advertised his gang affiliation like a bill board on Hollywood Boulevard. He possessed a menacing appearance even when he was smiling. While Black Jesus adopted more of a formal look, his little brother held to his street attire: oversized white Pro-Club under a gray hoodie, starched Ben Davis jeans and gray Nike Cortez. Black Jesus was the businessman and Bullet was the enforcer. He preferred to stay in the streets along with the rest of the soldiers, making sure the drug lord's presence was felt.

Before Gangsta could start over in Bullet's direction, Black Jesus' Dominican bodyguard, Tango, cut him off and gave him a thorough pat down that produced a chrome .45 automatic.

Bullet greeted Gangsta with a smile and a hug.

"What's up, papi?" He gave him the once over. "Looking all fly and shit."

Gangsta struck poses for Bullet, modeling what he was wearing. "Aye, what can I say?" he smiled brightly.

Tango offered Bullet Gangsta's gun but he waved him off.

"Fuck are you doing, dawg?" Bullet asked him. "This man has been doing business with us for many years. He's family. Give 'em his mothafucking gun back." Tango gave Gangsta his banger back. "Sorry about that, G, my bad. You know how this mothafucka is." he referred to the bodyguard's behavior.

"Don't even worry about it, Bullet," Gangsta stashed his burner on his person. "You know you're good money." He gave the young Vato a pound.

"And who is this?" Bullet asked, giving Vayda the once over. "Your date?"

"Yeah," Gangsta smiled like a shady cars salesman.

"What's your name, Gangsta's date?" Bullet inquired, kissing Vayda's hand.

"Vayda," The redbone replied.

"Pleasure to meet you, Vayda, you wouldn't by any chance have a twin sister, would you?"

"Nope, sweetie, I'm one of a kind."

"If it weren't for bad luck, I wouldn't have any luck at all." he said regretfully and turned his attention to the dance floor. "Aye, Jesus! Look whose here, homes! Check it out!"

Black Jesus spent around in his wheelchair and rolled over to his guests. He greeted Gangsta with a firm handshake and Vayda with a kiss on both cheeks. He then ushered them over to a table. "Wine?" Black Jesus asked Gangsta.

"Yeah, white," Gangsta replied, pulling out a chair for Vayda and then himself, sitting down.

"Ladies?" Black Jesus asked referring to the wine.

"White is fine," Vayda said.

"Okay, by me." The bronze skinned mami answered.

Black Jesus snapped his fingers and the waiter approached.

"Uh, Miguel," he addressed him. "White wine, quarto glasses, please."

He held up four fingers.

"Coming right up, boss," The waiter replied before turning to leave.

"Gracias," Black Jesus thanked him before turning to Gangsta. "So, Charles, how's business?" He addressed the O.G by the name on his birth certificate.

"Business is alright." He replied nonchalantly, shrugging his shoulders.

"Alright? Business is a lot more than alright. This is the millionth time I've met you in a suit; tailored at that. Calogero's, no?"

Gangsta nodded yes.

"Italian," Black Jesus exclaimed. "Expensive too, $5,000 dollars a suit, but what's money to guys like us?"

The waiter returned with a bottle of white wine and four glasses as requested. He sat a glass in front of each guest present at the table and poured the glasses half full.

"What will you fine people be having for dinner this evening." The waiter asked.

"Do you all mind?" Black Jesus raised a hand, looking around the table for anyone who objected him ordering their meals for them. Everyone agreed to let him order for them. Seeing that no one minded, he went on and ordered their meals in French. The waiter scribbled down the orders on a small tablet and then he headed off into the kitchen.

"Fucking show off," Gangsta leaned over and whispered to the drug lord before taking a sip of his wine.

"What?" Black Jesus asked, playing dumb.

"Mothafucka, you ordered our food in French and this is a Spanish restaurant."

"I'm afraid I have no idea of what you are referring to." He tried to contain a smile.

"Vayda, this nigga been doing this shit for years now; ever since we were in high school. Pretty Spanish mothafucka with the dark skin, and the Superman curl, laying down French, it was always enough to get this mothafucka laid." He took a sip of wine. "Rico Romance is what this fool use to call himself back in the day."

"Aye, what can I say?" Black Jesus said. "The chicas could never get enough of the Latin Lover." He did a funny little dance in his wheelchair. Everyone at the table busted up laughing. This rest of the night carried out just like this, two old friends reminiscing about old times and shooting on one another. When the food came they barely took two bites of it. The waiter had warmed their food up twice, but everyone was having such a good old time that they didn't pay any attention to their plates. Seeing that his guests weren't going to be getting to their meals any time soon, Black Jesus requested two doggy bags to go for them.

Usually Gangsta and Black Jesus never met up to make their exchange, but the drug lord wanted his old friend to come out to see his new restaurant so he obliged him. They both showed up in identical rentals. After the outing, Gangsta would leave in the car with the bricks stashed inside and one of Jesus' men would leave in the car with the money hidden in it. The transaction had been made like this for years.

Tipsy and thirty kilos richer, Gangsta and Vayda said their goodbyes and made their way for their vehicle. Vayda pushed the whip while Gangsta played the passenger seat. He placed a call to his nephews and told them that everything had gone smoothly and they were on their way back.

Forty minutes later

The front door of the trap house swung open and Gangsta and Vayda came dancing in over the threshold, hand and hand. They hummed the tune of the Spanish music that the El Mariachi band played back at Chico's. The pair moved around the living room as if they were competing in Dancing with the Stars. Unbeknownst to them, Pavielle stood in the bedroom doorway watching them as he took swigs from a bottle of Hennessy. He was shit faced drunk.

"I see y'all had yourselves a good old time." Pavielle's spoke, startling the dancing duo.

"Yes, we did," Vayda said, breaking her embrace from Gangsta. "It's been a long time since you've taken me out dancing. Why don't you dance with me?" she questioned, taking her man by the hand and moving from left to right, trying to get him to dance along with her.

"Gangstaz don't dance!" Pavielle told her, taking her by the face and locking lips with her. The entire time they were kissing he was staring at his uncle like '*Yeah, nigga, this is my bitch and don't you ever forget it.*' Vayda took the bottle of Hennessy from her man and took a long drink before passing it back to him.

"Alright, boo, I'm finna go hop in the shower." She told Pavielle and waved to his uncle, as she headed to the bedroom. He returned the gesture.

Gouch came out of his bedroom stretching and yawning with his head back, showcasing his teeth and every cavity in his mouth. He was in a wife beater and tan Dickie's, rubbing his flat, hairy stomach.

"I'm bored as fuck, y'all niggaz tryna get in a game of dominos?" he looked between his brother and uncle.

"Yeah, I could go for a game of bones." Gangsta replied. His forehead crinkled when he saw Pavielle eyeballing him and taking the occasional swallow of Hennessy.

"What about chu, bro?" Gouch tapped his sibling.

"I'm with it." He kept his eyes on their uncle as he took another swallow from his bottle.

"Bool, I'ma get the bones." He retreated to his bedroom to get the dominos so that they could play.

A few minutes later

Gangsta, Gouch and Pavielle sat at the kitchen table playing dominos. The entire time that Gouch and Gangsta were having a ball shooting the shit, the alcohol guerilla inside of Pavielle was pounding on its chest in a rage demanding to be let loose. It also didn't help that his mental was being assaulted with images of his uncle fucking the shit out of his woman. He got trailers of them sexing in his head and the more of them he saw the angrier he felt until, finally, he snapped like a twig.

"Stay the fuck away from my bitch!" A scowling Pavielle spat at his uncle, his words were like automatic gunfire. They came out abruptly, stopping Gangsta and Gouch's conversation.

The skin on Gangsta's forehead bunched together, hearing his youngest nephew get at him like that. Had it been anyone else he would have drew his banger and cracked his skull to the white meat with it.

"Excuse me." Gangsta frowned.

Pavielle leaned in closer to his uncle and repeated himself, "I said, Stay. The. Fuck. Away. From my bitch, nigga! You heard me, Hotlink!" Hotlink was a name given to Gangsta when he was in high school. He was known for running up in some of everything raw. And on more than one occasion he had gotten burned with an S.T.D, hence his nickname. Hotlink.

"You think I'm stupid?" Pavielle continued. "Nigga, I seen that shit earlier."

"Chill, Booby." Gouch tried to tell his little brother, placing a hand on his arm.

"Nah, fuck a chill, Gucci," Pavielle's face twisted and he snatched his arm away violently. "This old ass nigga ain't finna run up in my bitch! Not this nigga here!" He smacked his hand up against his chest hard with each word. "The rest of these niggaz running around here may be scared of him, but I'm not." he whipped out his .9mm, placed it on the table and leaned back in his chair, folding his arms to his chest. He mad dogged his uncle with the corner of his top lip twitching like an angry wolf.

"Blood, what the fuck is wrong with you?" Gouch snapped, looking at his brother like he'd lost his goddamn mind. "This is our fucking family!"

"This mothafucka ain't my family," Pavielle stared Gangsta dead in his eyes. The O.G held his gaze, clenching his muscular, veined fists firmly. "He's just a washed up, has-been gangsta, running around like he's in his twenties, tryna relive his glory days."

"Don't pay him any mind, unc. He's just drunk." Gouch defended his brother's actions.

"A drunken man speaks with a sober tongue."

Gangsta spoke, eyes still on Pavielle.

"Booby, you tripping," Gouch tried to snatch his brother's gun but he smacked his hand away.

"I'm not playing with you, Gucci! Don't touch my strap again, my nigga!" Pavielle turned his hateful eyes on his brother for a split second before returning them to his uncle. "So, how you wanna do this, old nigga? From the shoulders or with the tools?"

Gangsta turned to his sister's youngest son and said, "We can handle this shit from the shoulders!"

"Alright then, step outside." Pavielle went to rise and he fired on that ass. The young nigga winced and his neck bent at a funny angle, whipping around from the impact of the punch. His weight shifted in the chair and it went flying backwards, spilling him onto the floor, unconscious.

"He's knocked out cold, Gucci," Gangsta announced, looking at Pavielle snoring on the floor. "Help me get 'em on the couch." he and Gouch carried Pavielle into the living room and laid him on the couch. After draping a blanket over him, the O.G kneeled down to prop a pillow behind his head. "I don't know what I'm going to do with you, you crazy son of a bitch." He kissed him on the forehead and cut the lights out in the living room.

***

Pavielle woke up the next morning on the couch with a really bad hangover. He had no idea what had happened last night that left him with a sore jaw and Gangsta and Gouch didn't bother to remind him.

"Where's Lil' Gangsta? Fool was supposed to have been here this A.M." Pavielle asked as he whipped out his dick to take a piss.

"I don't know," Gangsta answered, shaving his head in the bathroom sink. With each naked strip he created on his head, he rinsed the shaver off under the faucet. "He was 'pose to have been here an hour ago."

"We've gotta hire better help." Pavielle glanced over his shoulder as he held his meat, relieving his bladder. "I know that's yo' dead homie's lil' brother and all, but damn!" he shook his head because Lil' Gangsta was a pitiful mothafucka who was more so a liability than an asset.

Lil' Gangsta was Big Gangsta's late homeboy, Tkay's, baby brother that had gotten murdered in a drive by a few years back. On a winter night, lying on the sidewalk, with

60

his blood pooling beneath him, he made Gangsta promise to look after his baby brother. Honoring the promise he made to his homeboy, Gangsta took his friend's younger brother under his wing, just as he did his own nephews.

"Let me worry about Lil' G," Gangsta said, washing traces of shaving cream from off his bald head. "You and Gouch drop off that product. That work ain't gone deliver its self."

"I'm on it, boss." Pavielle flushed the toilet and washed his hands. "You know momma got dialysis today, right?"

"Yeah, I'ma swing by there and drop her off once Lil' G get's here." He assured him.

"Alright then," Pavielle said, heading out of the bathroom.

***

Pavielle threw on a throwback 49niners jersey, a matching snapback and Levi's 501's. He then got Gouch from the other bedroom and they advanced on the front door. The brothers were to make their rounds to all five of
their uncle's trap houses, dropping off work.

Pavielle turned the knob and pulled open the door. To his surprise he found Lil' Gangsta with his fist raised about to knock. Scum was in the corners of the hoodlum's eyes and there was dry saliva around his mouth. You could tell he had awakened not too long ago.

Lil' Gangsta was a skinny, brown skinned cat with his hood tattooed all over his shaved head. He was known for playing with guns so niggaz gave him a wide berth.

"Blood, where the fuck have you been?" Pavielle scowled and twisted his lips. "Your ass was supposed to have been here, you're fucking up our money."

"My fault, Blood, I over slept."

"Nah, you over partied! You were over at the Fun Zone last night, getting high and fucking with the Swans. And don't try to lie, 'cause niggaz already told me."

"Damn, who the fuck are you, my P.O?" Lil'

Gangsta's forehead wrinkled, as he looked him up and down.

"Nah, homeboy," Pavielle shot back. "I'm the mothafucka that's gonna guarantee you have a closed casket if you don't hold it down." He lifted his jersey and exposed the Tec .9mm nestled in the front of his jeans.

"Whatever, my nigga," He waved him off and brushed past him into the house.

"Whatever my ass," Pavielle spat, "You betta keep that shit moving to the back where unc is."

"You don't like Blood do you?" Gouch asked him.

"Hell nah, fuck that nigga!"

Pavielle headed out of the front door with his brother bringing up the rear. Gouch closed the door behind them as they crossed the threshold.

***

When Lil' Gangsta walked into Gangsta's bedroom his big homie was getting dressed.

"Good morning, big homie." He greeted his O.G homie as he plopped down on the bed.

"You're late!" he told him, looking himself over in the mirror.

"I know, Blood, I over slept, my bad."

"Unh huh, you talk to that fool Pussy yet?"

"Man, hell naw!"

"I called Blood bix times; hit both of his bontacts. And he ain't never hit me back. I'm telling you, old boy is ducking us, real life. He doesn't have any intentions on paying us for that half a bird. You need to let me slide by

62

that fool's house and put this thang to work. You know what I'm saying? I don't know why you front that fool some work anyway, he's a crab."

"Money talks and bullshit walks." Gangsta proclaimed. "I'll do business with whomever if they

holding the right bag. Beef doesn't pay the mortgage or the car note."

"I heard that, but I don't know about doing business with enemies, though."

"Right," Gangsta replied, looping a gold necklace around his neck after sliding on a beautiful gold and diamond pinky ring. He studied his gear in the mirror while rubbing his jeweled hands together, biting down on his bottom lip. "We'll I'ma holla at Pussy, if he doesn't say what I wanna hear then we bringing them thangs out. You Griff me?"

"That's what the fuck I'm talking about," Lil' Gangsta exclaimed excitedly, whipping out a long nose .44 Magnum and a Glock .40. He pointed them bitches around

the room, visualizing busting at Pussy. "Bang, bang."

Later that night Gangsta had put in one last call to Pussy about the half of bird he had fronted him on consignment. Calling from his cell phone, he didn't receive an answer so he waited about an hour before using one of his workers cellulars; Pussy picked right up then.

"Big Time, what it do, my nigga?" Gangsta asked through the burn-out cellular pressed to his ear. "You're a hard man to get in touch with."

"A nigga been busy, loved one," Pussy replied, lying like a mothafucka. "What can I do for you, though?"

Gangsta was taken aback by how Pussy was acting, *surely this mothafucka knows he owes me for that half of bird,* he thought. *There's no way he forgot. What did he think? Half a brick of coke fell from the sky and landed in his lap? Nah, this nigga tryna play me. It's cool, though, I'ma just play along.*

"I've been trying to get a hold of you about that paper for that half." Gangsta told him.

"What half?" he played dumb.

Pussy was really wearing on Gangsta's nerves with his pretending to be dumb, but he maintained his composure.

"That half of that thang I fronted you a few weeks ago." he reminded him. The nigga didn't mean to speak so recklessly over the jack but old boy's playing dumb pissed him off.

"Oooooh, that half," Pussy pretended to recall. He knew exactly what half Gangsta was talking about. "Homie, I've been meaning to call you about that. My baby momma caught wind of me fucking around with my lil' young ho. Mannnnn, I come home and this bitch done keyed both of my cars; my X5 and my Benz. She cut up all my gear. My shoes, my leathers, the minks, and flushed that shit you gave me. Not to mention, some work of my own I had stashed. I must have beat that bitch half to death. A nigga almost caught his third strike and shit."

Gangsta was nobody's fool; he knew Pussy was capping him, trying to run that weak ass game.

"I hear that, Big Time, but what the fuck does that have to do with me?"

"Fuck you think it means? Charge it to the game, you bitch ass nigga!"

"On my momma, Pussy, if you don't come up off mine, I'ma…"

"You ain't gone do shit!" he cut him short. "Suck my dick, you bitch ass trick!"

He hung up on his ass.

In the hood, telling another man to suck your dick was a violation punishable by death. Gangsta had to answer the call or forfeit his reputation. If it got out that Pussy had strong armed some work from him then he would have to worry about every two-bit hustler trying to pull the same scheme. And he couldn't allow that, because in his business ones reputation was everything. He could have easily sent some of his hitters by Pussy way to lay his ass down, but due to the disrespect and his ego, Gangsta decided to answer back himself. It had been five years since he had killed something and he thought this was the perfect time to bring his strap out of retirement.

The next night

Gangsta and Lil' Gangsta stalked Pussy to the Westside. On the way over they missed their chance to burn him at a red light on Slauson and Western. Gangsta had pointed his burner out of the driver side window at him and was about to blow the nigga'z noddles out of his head, when he spotted a police cruiser coming up beside them. Right then he thought that nigga Pussy had a guardian angel watching over him. And if this was the case then he was lucky that he couldn't see him, because if he could he would have blasted on his mothafucking ass, too.

The gangstas decided to keep following their prey until another opportunity presented its self. And so they found themselves at the Barbary Coast in the city of Gardena off of Western Avenue. Gangsta parked on a residential street, eight cars down from Western Avenue. He and his accomplice slumped low in the seats of his Cutlass Supreme, keeping their eyes glued to the entrance of the establishment. They were dressed in black from head to toe. Gangsta gripped a long nose .357 Magnum and his protégé clutched a Glock .40 with an extended magazine. So far the pair had spent a total of four hours staking out the Barbary Coast waiting for Pussy to make his exit. Lil' Gangsta had grown impatient. All of his bitching and complaining was getting on his big homie's nerves. The nigga acted like they were picking up a couple of girls for a drive-in movie and they were taking too long to come outside.

"Fuuuck!" Lil' Gangsta vented his frustration. He ran his hand down his face and blew hot air. "When this nigga gone show his ugly ass face so I can blow that bitch off, Blood?"

"See, that's the problem with you young niggaz today. You don't have any patience. Haven't you heard of the phrase, 'Good things come to those who wait?'"

"Yeah, and?"

"Why don't chu try applying some of that philosophy to this here situation."

"Whatever!" Lil' Gangsta waved his big homie off. "What chu think they doing in there anyway?"

"The same thing you and I would be doing if we were in there; drinking, smoking and hollering at hoes."

"Sheeeiiiit, I know that's right." He gave him a pound.

"Shhhh," Gangsta held a finger to his lips. "I think that's him." He nodded to the windshield at a man exiting the gentlemen's club with two strippers.

"Yeah, that's his bitch ass," Lil' Gangsta smiled evilly and rubbed his gloved hands together in anticipation of the chaos that they were about to create. "Nigga just like Jesus, he might not be there when you want 'em, but he's always on time." He checked the magazine of his weapon and then smacked it back into the bottom of it, cocking that bitch.

Gangsta closed the chamber of his revolver after making sure it was fully loaded. "Let's throw this nigga a farewell party." he pulled the bandana up over his mouth and so did Lil' Gangsta. They hopped out of the Cutlass and shut their doors quietly behind them. Hunching over on their knees, they moved in on the Barbary Coast like a military trained unit.

***

Pussy's Pimp C looking ass made his way out of the thick Oakwood door of the Barbary Coast with a beezy under each arm. It didn't take much convincing to get two of the strip clubs most popular dancers to come home with him, especially since he'd been making it rain and popping five hundred dollar bottles of champagne since he'd gotten there. With the promise of them both leaving his condo a stack richer than they were before they left the strip club, they were all for the private performance he was bartering for.

Pussy was a chubby light skinned dude who wore gold frames, several necklaces and a diamond pinky ring.

On top of his dome there was a Chinchilla hat which he'd worn with a matching jacket. The hefty stud looked more like a throwback to pimps of the 1970's exploitation films than the neighborhood dope man that he actually was. He was drunk and high, but had more than enough sense for the freaky shit he planned on doing to the girls once he got them back to his pad.

"Unh uh," he looked from each of his conquests' ample asses, licking his lips and shaking his head. His chunky ass couldn't wait to get them alone and all to himself. The thought alone had his dick nudging his zipper. The girls rested their heads on his shoulders. One slipped her hand between the buttons of his shirt and rubbed on his hairy chest while the other groped his hardness through the fabric of his slacks. Feeling him stiffen further, she brought her

67

head up and kissed him deep and hungrily. They could hear one another's saliva sloshing around in the other's mouth. When Pussy took his lips from the first girl and started locking lips with the other, he saw something that made his eyes bulge in his fucking head. Two niggaz dressed in all black were hurrying across the street with their burners at their sides. Their lethal eyes were set on him so he already knew what fucking time it was.

"Oh, shit!" Pussy shoved the broad that he was kissing before Gangsta. He went to draw his own heat but grabbed air, remembering that he'd left it under the driver's seat of his Benz, because he wouldn't gain access to the gentlemen's club with it. With that in mind, he turned around and broke back to the door of the establishment with a terrified look on his face.

The broad that he shoved before his predator stumbled forward, but recovered her balance on her high heel pumps, only to lock eyes with the buff nigga with the shiny revolver. His tool gleamed under the light post's illumination as he lifted it up, pointing its deadly end at her. Her eyes bugged and she went to scream so he made her swallow a bullet, splattering a gaping, gooey hole at the back of her dome piece. She collapsed lifelessly right where she stood.

"Ahhhhh! Ahhhhh!" the other broad took off running as fast as she could in a pair of clear bottom stilettos and a tight leopard print dress.

"Get that bitch, no witnesses." Gangsta ordered, pointing his pistol in the fleeing woman's direction. "She doesn't make it off of this block, you hear me? She doesn't make it off this block!" With the command given, Lil' Gangsta took off after old girl moving like a track star, burner in hand. They both disappeared alongside the building. Gangsta didn't even flinch when he heard the rapid gunfire that resonated throughout the night. He already knew that his little homie had earned himself his fourth teardrop.

Bloc! Bloc! Bloc! Bloc!

"Wait, wait…" Pussy called out to the bouncer that was hurriedly slamming the door so the drama wouldn't find its way inside of the club. He'd almost reached the closing door when his calves exploded one by one, causing him to fall to the sidewalk. He hit the ground hard as a mothafucka wincing. Groaning, he pulled himself along dragging his legs with him. When he looked over his shoulder he saw Gangsta approaching with the smoking steel in his hand. Pussy's heart pounded inside of his chest and his eyes became as big as saucers. He struggled to move forth, breaking a sweat and causing beads to run down his forehead. A shadow eclipsed him and he felt Gangsta's boot mash down on his wounded leg. He hollered out in excruciation so the O.G took his foot off him.

"Turn yo' ho ass over, nigga!" Gangsta ordered him, leveling his banger down at his punk ass.

Pussy slowly turned over moaning in agony. He looked alive once he found himself staring down his enemy's hollowed barrel. He swallowed the ball of nervousness in his throat and shut his eyelids for a moment before peeling them back open. His heart pounded inside of his chest but he had to calm down, because he didn't want to leave this world like a mark. The G in him was reborn. He would face his certain death with bravery.

"I'll see you in hell." He scowled and squared his jaws, vein bulging at his temple.

"Take these with you!" Gangsta snarled and pulled the trigger, causing the chamber of his revolver to spin. Each time his weapon fired a golden orange illumination shone on his scowling face.

Blam! Blam! Blam! Blam!

Pussy's dome exploded like a rotten pumpkin hitting the ground from a fifty foot fall. There was no way in hell that the dope man would get an open casket funeral now. Gangsta took the time to admire his handiwork before stuffing his warm weapon into the front of his jeans. Hearing hurried footsteps and heavy breathing, he looked to the corner of the establishment. He saw Lil' Gangsta's shadow as he was running toward him. The young nigga darted out into the street motioning for him to follow. The O.G took off right behind him. They recovered their G-ride, busted a U-turn on the residential street, and left in the opposite direction of which they came.

Just another 187.

Chapter Five

"Take this mothafucka over to those factories over there on

11th avenue and torch it," Gangsta told Lil' Gangsta from the passenger seat as the Cutlass idled out in the alley behind his mother's house. "Wipe them straps down and get rid of them. I don't care if you toss'em in a lake or bury 'em. Just get rid of them mothafuckaz, we don't need anything connecting us to them bodies over there, you Griff me?"

Lil' Gangsta nodded his understanding.

"Call me once this shit is done." Gangsta handed him his strap and hopped out of the car. He made his way to is mother's house as his little homie drove off down the alley.

Turning out onto Central Avenue from the alley, Lil' Gangsta smiled like the cat that had swallowed the canary. He was ecstatic about having carried out a mission with his big homie Gangsta, the urban legend. To him, putting in work with the O.G was an honor, a memory to cherish for a life time. It was right up there with shaking hands with the president.

Thirty minutes later

Lil' Gangsta ran down the block as the G-ride caught flames and then exploded, scattering burning wreckage everywhere. Turning the corner at the end of the avenue, he pulled the .357 from his hoodie with his bandana and dropped it into the gutter. A fire truck with its sirens blaring blew past him in a hurry. He was just about to dump his Glock when he saw an unmarked police car pulling up. He quickly sat on the bus-stop bench and played the role of a pedestrian waiting on his ride. The unmarked car pulled up and his stomach twisted in knots as his eyes met those of Detectives Arsenegger and Ortiz. He was familiar with the crooked law enforcers and their reputations as they were with his.

"What's up, Jerome?" Arsenegger addressed Lil' Gangsta by his government name with a sinister smile, showcasing all thirty two of his straight, white teeth. He had jet black hair, ocean blue eyes and a five o'clock shadow. You could tell by his sixteen inch biceps and washboard stomach that the gym was a second home to him.

"What's up, Blood?" Lil' Gangsta responded behind a scowl. He was putting up a front though, because he was scared as shit.

"Long time, no see," Ortiz threw his head back like What's up? He was Puerto Rican but as equally as scandalous as his Australian partner. He sported a shaved head and a muscular physique.

"Not long enough." Lil' Gangsta retorted under his breath, looking down the block as if he was waiting for the bus to arrive.

"What chu got there, my nigga?" Arsenegger asked before taking a sip from his cup of coffee. He noticed the hoodlum had his hands stashed in the large pocket of his hoodie which was odd because it wasn't that cold outside.

"Shit." Lil' Gangsta replied nonchalantly.

"Oh, you got something, little man!" Arsenegger said, swinging open the passenger side door. As soon as Lil' Gangsta saw him plant a foot on the pavement, he broke up the avenue. "Mothafucka," Arsenegger fumed, throwing his cup of coffee and hopping back into the passenger seat. The cup deflected off of the curb and spilled the hot liquid everywhere. Ortiz floored the Crown Victoria and hit the sirens, speeding toward their suspect.

The Crown Victoria mowed down a water hydrant and sent a geyser of water into the air. A stray cat shot out from the path of the speeding car like a bolt of lightning, looking like a blur. A homeless man pushing a shopping cart saw the car heading his way; he dove out of its way, missing it by a foot.

Boom!

The shopping cart went up in the air, spilling its contents. All of its items came raining down upon the pavement. Lil' Gangsta bent the corner of the block and ran into an alley, with the Crown Victoria in hot pursuit. The unmarked car lit up the trashy alley as it barreled after the hoodlum, trying to catch up to him.

"You want me to mow this mothafucka down!" Ortiz looked to Arsenegger. The alley's walls looked like flashes of gray as the Crown Victoria sped down the path so fast.

"Nah, just shake his little punk ass up," Aresenegger told him. Ortiz quickly closed the distance between his vehicle and their suspect.

Boom!

"Ughhh." Lil' Gangsta went over the hood of the Crown Victoria and rolled off it, crashing to the ground. His Glock went spiraling across the ground in circles until it bumped up against a pile of black trash bags. Arsenegger and Ortiz hopped out of the unmarked car and casually made their way over to their suspect who was sprawled out on the ground, groaning in pain.

"Uuuuh," Lil' Gangsta moved his head from side to side, wincing. He was hurting like a mothafucka.

"Where were you off to in such a rush, Blood?" Arsenegger smiled and kicked him in the side causing him to grimace. He rolled over holding his side, groaning.

"Well, look what we've got here."Ortiz smiled evilly. When Arsennegger looked to his partner he was holding up their suspect's Glock by the trigger guard with an ink pen.

Lil' Gangsta raised his head to see what the crooked law enforcer had on him. Once he saw it was his gun, he let his head drop to the ground.

"Ah, fuck me!" he spat.

Arsenegger smiled and said to him, "That's yo' ass!"

Right after, he was pulling his handcuffs from around his back to cuff him.

An hour later

Gangsta sat on the couch watching *The Godfather* on cable TV while eating a bowl of Cookies & Cream and Rainbow Sherbet ice cream. He was in his sleep wear: a black Pro-Club, tan Dickie shorts and black corduroy house shoes. He glanced up at the cable box; its digital clock read 2:00 A.M; well into the next morning. Lil' Gangsta was supposed to have called him after he got rid of the guns and disposed of the G-ride. Four hours had passed since his little homie had dropped him off and he hadn't heard a word from him. He'd been blowing his cell phone up for the past two and a half hours but never received an answer. He had a feeling something was wrong but he hoped that it was just paranoia.

"Man, I wish you would have let me and Gucci get down on that lil' situation with Pussy for you," Pavielle said from the reclining chair as he took pulls of a Kush blunt; his eyes were bloodshot red and glassy. "You're a boss; you've got soldiers in these streets to put that work in."

"Yeah, I know," Gangsta sat the empty bowl onto the table. "But that mothafucka was so disrespectful, I had to get at 'em myself, or I wouldn't be able to sleep at night." "I

Griff you; what's done is done. All you can do is put this shit behind you and move on."

"No doubt. I just wish Lil' Gangsta would hit me back though, gotta nigga on edge. I should have sent you or Gucci with him."

"Yeah, 'cause niggaz like that will fuck up a wet dream," Pavielle blew smoke rings into the air. "I never did like that lil' mothafucka, man, it's something about his lil' punk ass."

Silence fell between the two men and before Pavielle knew it, his uncle was fast asleep. Seeing this, he murdered the TV with the remote control, draped his jacket over Gangsta and killed the lights before heading into his bedroom.

Early as shit the next morning

Boom! Boom! Boom! Boom!

Gangsta awoke startled, hearing the front door rattle with such brute force. "Who the fuck is it?!" he called out from the couch.

"Police, motherfucker!" a voice rang from the opposite side of the door. "Open up!"

Gangsta sprung to his feet, hobbled over to the window as fast as he could and took a peek out of the curtains. There were about eight police cars outside on the street. A dozen police officers were on the lawn, some of them had K-9s but they all were packing some very serious firepower.

Gangsta turned around and found Pavielle, Vayda, and Gouch standing behind him, they all were groggily from sleep.

"Blood, who the fuck is that?" Gouch asked, wiping the scum from his eyes.

"Shhh," Gangsta hushed his oldest nephew, holding a finger to his lips. "Be quiet, it's the mothafucking cops!"

"Ah, shit!" Gouch cursed.

"Say what?" Pavielle asked, hearing the police mentioned snapped him out of his grogginess.

"Booby, Gucci, y'all niggaz stash the straps. Vayda," Gangsta addressed the redbone. "Go get momma up."

The pounding continued on the door, as the trio split up to complete their tasks. Pavielle and Gouch stashed the straps that they kept in the house in a secret stash spot inside of the attic. They then returned to the living room where they found Vayda, G-momma and their uncle waiting.

"Alright, mommy, Vay, Booby, Gucci," Gangsta addressed his family. "Everybody put their hands up and keep 'em up. When these people bust up in here, don't make any sudden moves. Do exactly what they say, when they say it!" he looked to his mother. "You got it, mommy?"

"Yes, but I wish someone would tell me what's going on here, Cha Cha?" G-momma called him by his childhood nickname, a pleaded with a worried expression.

"No time to explain, ma." He kissed his mother on her forehead and headed to the door. Looking back at his family he took a deep breath before going about the task of opening up the door. As soon as he finished unlocking and unchaining it, the police came flooding in over the threshold. They directed everyone down on their bellies with their hands behind their heads so they could cuff them.

The police tore the house up looking for guns and drugs, but they found neither. Once they were done with their search the place looked like a tornado had been through it. The police released everyone from their metal bracelets except Gangsta; they were bringing him down to the precinct. He was wanted for questioning behind a few homicides. Hearing '*Homicides*' mentioned made the O.G heart skip a beat. He already knew what was up; Lil' Gangsta had gotten pinched and had dropped a dime on him. That's why he never called him back last night. It was just too coincidental.

When the police led Gangsta outside in handcuffs the entire neighborhood looked like it was out. You would have thought the president of the United States was going to roll through the hood that gloomy morning. Gangsta kept a broad smile on his face as he was led to a police car. As the police car pulled off, he looked out the back window to his mother and mouthed "I love you". G-momma wiped the tears from her eyes and mouthed the words back.

***

Lil' Gangsta stepped out of the Newton Division precinct a nervous wreck. He pulled his hoodie over his head as he made his way down the steps of the police station. Making his way upon the sidewalk, he observed all of his surroundings before lighting up a Newport. He pulled smoke into his lungs and unleashed it into the world in the form of a cloud.

Arsenegger and Ortiz had his nuts in a vice grip so he had two choices: keep his mouth shut and ride the bullet, or turn state's evidence. Lil' Gangsta took the ladder. He opted to become a witness for the state and in exchange he was promised a shorter sentence.

Being a rat was frowned upon in his hood and many hoods across the globe, but to Lil' Gangsta, it was a small price to pay for his freedom. He could live with being a snitch but he couldn't live with spending the rest of his life behind bars. Though he did sign the affidavit, it was no way in hell he was getting on the stand to testify against Gangsta.

He couldn't bring himself to look him in the eyes after stabbing him in the back; especially after all he had done for him.

A forest green Ford Escort pulled up in front of the police station. Lil' Gangsta took one last pull of his cancer stick, flicked it and hopped in. The little car pulled off, taking the Y.G with it and leaving his misdeeds behind.

Meanwhile

Gangsta sat in the claustrophobic interrogation room down at Newton Division police station, picking the scum out of his finger nails. For the past three and a half hours Detectives Arsenegger and Ortiz had been hitting him with a barrage of questions, to which he shrugged his shoulders and answered "*I don't know*" to.

"Like I told y'all the first fifty million times," Gangsta began. "I don't know shit about any bodies dropping way over on the westside. I'm from the eastside, baby."

"Bullshit!" Ortiz called him on his lie, slamming his fist down on the table. He was trying to scare the O.G but had been failing miserably since the interrogation started.

"Hmmm, I beg to differ." Gangsta grinned. All this shit that the crooked badges were trying to pull he had been through it a hundred times already. Needless to say, he knew how to handle himself in such a situation.

"Listen, asshole," Arsenegger began, rolling up his sleeves and then sitting down on the table. "You're not fooling us with this line of bullshit you keep trying to feed us, we know for a fact that you were involved with those murders. Your little homeboy, Lil' Gangsta," Gangsta's eyes wandered up from his nails and met the detective's. "I thought that might ring a bell, told us everything. We threw some numbers at him and he gave it up faster than a Thai hooker."

"Is that right?" Gangsta said nonchalantly, one eyebrow lifted.

"You bet," Arsenegger said. "His little punk ass gave you a death sentence. You hopped in the electric chair, we strapped you down, but he for damn sure raised the lever." Gangsta blew hard and rolled his eyes to their whites.

"Luckily for you I'm feeling very generous today. I'm in a good mood. So, I'm gonna give you a chance to confess so we can see about working out some kind of deal here for you. What do you say, big man? Help me to help you."

Gangsta looked like he had the weight of the world on his shoulders. He blew hard and said, "Think I can bum a cigarette off of you detective?"

Upon hearing the O.G's request, Arsenegger and Ortiz exchanged shit-eating-grins. A suspect asking for a cigarette during an interrogation usually meant he or she was ready to confess their sins and needed the nicotine to calm their nerves. Arsenegger gave Gangsta a cigarette and lit it with a struck match, fanning out the flame of it. He tossed the used match into the waste basket and posted up beside his partner. They watched as Gangsta took two long pulls of the cancer stick and then blew smoke, polluting the atmosphere.

"What kind of deal do you think you can work out for me?" Gangsta looked from Arsenegger to Ortiz.

"The sweetest one you've ever heard of, big dawg." Arsenegger assured him. "I'm talking about two, three years…tops."

He lied through his fucking teeth.

"Alright," Gangsta said, taking two more pulls of the cigarette he was given. He mashed the Joe out in the ashtray on the table, clearing his throat. The snake ass detectives smiled and gave each other a pound. "You two crooked ass mothafuckaz can suck my dick!" Gangsta started off, looking between the two devils. Detective Arseneggers smile gave way to a mask of hatred and he found himself clenching his jaws. "Y'all got me fucked up, I'm Big Gangsta from Eastside 20s!Lock me up and throw away the key, but when it's all said and done, they gone bury me a G!"

Arsenegger leapt over the table and started choking Gangsta, but Ortiz pulled him off. The interrogation room's door swung open and four uniformed officers rushed in to help Ortiz restrain his partner.

"Hahahahahahaha," Gangsta sat in the iron-chair laughing his ass off, he got a kick out of getting under the detective's skin.

"You fucking, nigger," Arsenegger shouted, spit flying from off his lips. His eyes were bloodshot and glassy as fuck. Veins were webbed on his temples and neck. "I'm going to see to it that they gas your black ass! Then I'm going to go after your entire fucking family! And I'm going to bury them in the fucking ground! And then I'm going to go after your whole crew! You hear me, you black son of a bitch?" he screamed, struggling to break free from the uniformed cops and his partner.

"Hahahahahaha," Gangsta laughed harder and louder, taunting the racist detective.

"Get this piece of shit out of here!" Ortiz told the uniformed cops.

Two police officers pulled Gangsta to his feet, handcuffed him and led him out of the interrogation room laughing like a maniac.

"Hahahahahaha."

Chapter Six

"You ever hear back from unc?" Gouch asked Pavielle from the kitchen, he was sitting at the table practicing rolling with a pair of red dice.

"Not yet," Pavielle answered. He was sprawled out on the couch taking down his hair. "He said he was going to call once he got his hands on a burn-out. He doesn't wanna talk on the jack they have in there, you know they be recording niggaz conversations and shit."

"Yeah, I know, has anything changed with his bail?" Gouch schooled the dice.

"Hell naw, they haven't set a bail amount."

"Man, I swear to God, Blood, if I ever run across bitch-boy I'm a split his shit to the white meat."

"There still ain't no word on Lil' Gangsta?"

"Nah, ain't no word on that fuck-nigga, all the homies saying he fled the hood," Gouch informed him. "And if he's smart, the rat bastard will stay gone."

"I told unc I didn't like that lil' nigga, man, it was always something about him. But you can't tell Gangsta shit, that nigga stubborn than a mothafucka." Gouch laughed and Pavielle side eyed him. "The fuck is so funny?"

"Look who's talking."

Pavielle gave Gouch the finger, just then, his cell phone rang. Pavielle picked the burn-out up from his lap and looked at the caller ID. He didn't recognize the number displayed but he assumed it was his uncle. "I think this is him." He sat up on the couch, pressed *talk* and brought the phone to his ear.

Gouch plopped down on the couch beside Pavielle.

"Hello?" Pavielle spoke into the burn-out.

"What's up, Booby?" Gangsta said into the cellular.

"Ain't shit, out here handling your business, how are you, though?"

"I'm alright, taking it one day at a time, nephew. How are mommy and Gucci doing?"

"They're straight. Momma is at dialysis and Gucci is right here, you wanna speak to him?"

"Nah, I can rap with Gucci later, I wanted to talk to you."

"What's on your mind?"

"I'm gonna let chu run the chicken shack for me. Hell, it ain't like I can run it from inside of here."

Gangsta was speaking in code. He was actually taking about Pavielle running his operation while he was on lock. The young nigga was blood, and more qualified than anyone he could think of to handle his business. Hell, he'd been grooming him for this day.

"You're talking brazy right now, unc! You'll be home in a hot minute. We got Goldberg on your case. He ain't ever lost a case for us. That old Jew is the D.A's worst nightmare."

"I don't know, Booby, shit not looking so good for me. We'll see, though. This shit is in God's hands now."

"Amen!"

"Like I was saying though, I'ma let chu run the business and make sure everything is okay. You'll have Gucci to watch your back so you'll be straight. Two heads are always better than one, you Griff me? I've already talked to the dude that supplies me with all of the meat I use. He's got beef, pork, and whole chickens. I'm talking about pure birds too. None of that shit that's shot full of those hormones."

"Alright, how do I get in touch with him?"

"Homie's busy, real busy.He told me he'll get in touch with you soon, though. Just make sure you answer yo' jack 'cause you don't want him thinking something else. 'Cause then you'll have to go find someone else that you'll have to get the meat from and I'm positive that they won't give you a price as sweet as him."

What Gangsta was actually saying was that if Pavielle didn't answer the plug's call then he'd probably think that something fishy was going on. And if he did he'd sever ties, leaving him to find someone else to buy his drugs from.

"Bool, we're going to bring momma up there to see you Friday."

"Alright, Booby, y'all stay up. I love y'all."

"We love you, too, unc."

"Twenty minutes." He hung up.

Elsewhere

Bullet shook his head at the bad news that had just been laid on him; he wiped his mouth with a napkin cloth and cleared his throat.

"How much time is he looking at?" he asked Black Jesus, who was sitting at the opposite end of the dining room table.

"Life." he replied, pouring himself a glass of red wine. "I'm really disappointed with Charles; he wasn't supposed to get his hands dirty. Guys like us have clean-up crews on our payrolls to handle matters like this. Shooting in the middle of the ghetto like some common thug is not how you handle business."

"What are you talking about, bro? Gangsta brought it to those fools how a gangster is supposed to."

"Gangster?" Black Jesus stopped his wine glass at his lips.

"There's nothing gangster about spending the rest of your life behind the wall, or being gassed like some diseased rodent. You've got a lot to learn about life, little brother." He took a swallow of wine.

Bullet nodded his head in agreement, his big brother made a good point. There wasn't anything "Gangster" about spending the rest of your life in prison, or being sentenced to death. But if he had a choice in the matter, he'd rather take the short walk to his execution, than rot behind a barbwire fence.

"So, what exterminator should we hire?" Bullet inquired. "I was thinking about Tito." He took a bite of salmon.

"Definitely not, Tito's family," Black Jesus told him.

"We don't want this thing being traced back to us. It's bad enough the cops are sniffing around. The last thing I want to do is give them a reason to come prying further in my affairs. We'll get some outside assistance for our little vermin."

"Who did you have in mind?"

The drug lord held up his fork, as he chewed his food and then he swallowed. "The Ghost," he went back to cutting up his salmon.

"The Ghost?"

"Unh huh," Black Jesus said, munching on salmon.

"You sure you wanna use this guy? I mean, he charges an arm and a leg."

"Fifty thousand dollars to be exact, but who gives a shit? I have more money than I know what to do with. I spend fifty thousand dollars a year on socks and drawers alone. What the fuck do I care?" Black Jesus was about to take another bite of salmon until he noticed how uptight

Bullet was at the mention of hiring the infamous hit-man.

"You know, if I didn't know any better, I'd think old Ghost had you spooked."

"Who me?" his brows furrowed as he pointed his thumb at his chest, "Not the kid, my heart don't pump no Kool-Aid, you know my resume." He took a sip of red wine.

Bullet was full of shit; the hit-man gave him the creeps. As a kid he was told stories about the assassin as if he were The Boogie Man.

Black Jesus clapped his hands sporadically and the maid emerged in the dining room with a pearl and gold antique telephone on a golden platter. It was time to make a very important phone call.

That night

A milk white stretch Mercedes Benz pulled up on 124th and Compton Avenue. The chauffeur slid out from behind its wheel, popped its trunk and removed a wheelchair. He sat the wheelchair on the ground, closed the trunk and proceeded around to the back passenger door. He then opened the back door of the vehicle and helped Black Jesus into the confines of the wheelchair. Tango exited the limo from the opposite side and made his way over to his boss. He took his wheelchair by the handles and rolled him upon the sidewalk. Rolling Black Jesus through the black iron-gate of the house, he gave the creepy looking place a once over and could have sworn he saw a dark figure move past the openings of one of its boarded up windows.

Tango knocked on the chipped wood door of the old house and paint chips floated into the crisp, cold night air. For a moment there was silence, and then they heard what sounded like ten locks coming undid. The front-door swung inward and Tango and Black Jesus' nasal passages were assaulted by an odor so foul that it made them gag. The stench was a combination of blood, sweat, urine and feces. Tango and Black Jesus brandished their handkerchiefs and covered their noses. As they proceeded over the threshold the front door slammed shut behind them, locking. Startled, Tango pulled his gun and stepped in front of his boss to shield him from any danger. He pointed his banger and turned his head in every direction a threat might present itself.

Black Jesus looked around the living room; its hardwood floors were dirty and wore gaping holes. Its walls and ceiling was filthy and covered in green mole from water damage.

"Hello? My name is Jesus Arturo!" Black Jesus called out. "I'm looking for the one they call The Ghost!" he spoke loud enough for anyone to hear that may be listening.

"Come down into the basement!" A voice came from the dirty, spider webbed intercom on the wall. The voice was deep with a heavy bass to it. If you were to close your eyes you could assume that it belonged to a great and powerful entity.

Tango and Black Jesus' eyes darted all around the living room trying to figure out where the voice had come from. Giving up, they moved in on the basement door. Tango twisted the door knob and pushed in on it with his shoulder but it wouldn't budge. He then tackled the door twice which caused debris to fall from the ceiling. Giving it another try, he took a few steps back, ran forth and threw his body toward the door. Before the door and his 200 lb frame could meet, it swung open and he went tumbling down a flight of steps. The Dominican bodyguard hit the basement floor and his gun went skidding into the wall.

Black Jesus rolled into the doorway and looked down the flight of steps that lead into the basement. The steps were dusty and looked weak, as if they'd give under the slightest pressure.

"Tango, are you okay?" Black Jesus called down to him.

"Yeah," Tango responded, rubbing the lump forming on his head and surveying the basement.

"Who's down there?"

"No one," he answered, picking up his banger from against the wall. "It's hot as hell, though. There's a burning furnace down here!"

"Alright, I'm going to try to come down!" With that said, the wooden steps converted into a ramp, easily accessible for a wheelchair. "Was that you who did that?!"

"No!" Tango said, looking around the basement with his black steel out stretched, ready to open fire on anyone posing a threat.

"Alright, I'm coming down!" the drug lord rolled himself down the ramp and onto the basement floor beside his bodyguard. Standing side by side, they looked over the basement; it was clean as a whistle.

"Fuck is going on here?" Tango asked, forehead creased, "Where is your hit-man?"

"Ghost," Black Jesus called out. "Hola, mi amigo, I've come to talk business!" He rolled his wheelchair an inch forward and a wild German shepherd shot from out of the dark corner of the basement. The huge dog leapt forward and tried to bite the Mexican drug lord's face off, but it was snagged in mid air by the chain attached to the collar around its neck. The German shepherd snarled and barked at Tango and Black Jesus. Tango raised his weapon and was just about to fire on the dog when he heard a voice from the darkness.

"Hank!" The voice erupted from the confines of the shadows. "Sit your ass down!" An albino man oozed from the shadows of the basement. He had dark menacing eyes and long blonde hair that lay over his broad shoulders. His six foot two frame was lean and mean, with just the right amount of muscle. He was in a black long brim hat, a cape and needle pointed boots with silver, gleaming spurs on the heels of them. The Ghost bit into a juicy peach as he ascended on the drug lord and his bodyguard. He seemed to more so float over than walk. This was just one of the attributes to which why he was christened, *The Ghost.*

The Ghost was so tall that his shadow gave his guests shade. Tango's eyes crept up from his boots and settled into the cold eyes of the pale skinned assassin. The Dominican was intimidated by the killer but he wouldn't let it show. He had a reputation made of Teflon and he refused to relinquish any dents to it.

The Ghost's eyes wandered from Tango's and rested on Black Jesus'. He shrugged his shoulders and said, "So, talk," before taking another bite of his peach.

"Right," Black Jesus said, popping the locks on his briefcase. He raised the lid and revealed rows of crisps $5,000 stacks. On top of the bills was a black & white photograph of Lil' Gangsta. He removed the photograph from the briefcase and handed it over to the hit-man.

"His government, alias and current address are on the back." Black Jesus informed him "Though I doubt you'll find him there."

The Ghost smacked the imaginary crumbs from his palms and tossed his half eaten peach high over his shoulder. Hank leapt into the air like a dolphin, snagged it and gobbled it down. The assassin sucked the juices of the ripe fruit from his fingers as he studied the information on the back of the photograph.

"Is that my money?" he asked, pointing to the briefcase on the drug lord's lap.

"Yes, it's all here, fifty thousand dollars," Black Jesus told him. The Ghost closed the briefcase and picked it up from Black Jesus' lap. He didn't even bother to check the dollar amount. "Don't you want to make sure the money is all there?"

"Oh, it's all there." The Ghost said confidently.

"How can you be so sure?" a line indented his forehead.

"Because no one has ever been stupid enough to cross The Ghost," He spoke of himself in third person. Tango was about to make a move on the assassin for his comment, but his boss waved him off.

"Down, boy," The Ghost flashed the bodyguard a devilish grin, showcasing the fang like teeth inside of his mouth. He then looked to Black Jesus. "How do you want 'em," he held up the photograph of Lil' Gangsta "Open or closed casket?"

"Do as you please. Just as long as you put him out of his misery," he told him. "I trust that you still have my number."

"No more phones, I'll be contacting you directly."

"Don't run off with that money and make me come looking for you." Tango warned the assassin, as he rolled his boss over to the ramp. The Ghost laughed at his threat; he knew the bodyguard was no match for his talents. The albino was a proficient killer and was in incredible shape. He would make short work of the old gangster if they were to bump heads.

"Don't tempt me." The Ghost smiled wickedly.

"You think this clown is going to come through?" Tango asked his employer as he rolled him up the ramp.

"Oh, he'll deliver," Black Jesus told him, lighting up a cigar and blowing out smoke. "There's no doubt in my mind."

You can take that to the bank, he thought.

Chapter Seven

Fat Travon was posted up in front of Ace's mini market curb serving. He had both of his hands in his jacket; in one pocket he held onto a .32 and in the other he grasped a fist full of ten dollar crack rocks. Paranoid, every five seconds he found himself looking over his shoulders, checking his surroundings. He knew he had no business hustling on Adams; it had been made clear that this was Big Gangsta's territory. Therefore, the small piece of land was off limits to any homies who weren't under the shot caller's employ. But things had changed since Gangsta had gotten locked up and gave his nephew the imaginary deed to the property. It was no longer Gangsta's land he was slinging on, but O.G Booby Loco's. And to him the differences were considerable.

Travon knew of Booby and his older brother Gouch's reputations. But he didn't care, he had a family to support and neither O.G Booby nor his brother was going to put food in his babies' mouths. He had rent for two houses, two car notes, five kids, three baby mommas and his mother's medical bills to take care of.

The Adams block was the best strip for a D-boy to get his hustle on; the block was a gold mine for corner hustlers. You could always catch a few fiends sniffing around for a fix. Travon had only been posted up for an hour and had clocked $300 dollars already. The hell if he was going to pack it up and move somewhere else to hustle just because Bobby said so. Fuck that, he was strapped; he was going to hold his little corner down and go to war behind it if necessary. If shit got too hot he had a couple of riders he could call to bear arms alongside him.

A Beach Cruiser skidded to a stop beside Fat Travon, the stubby man spun around and tried to pull his banger but it got snagged in the inside of his jacket's pocket. After the slip up, he was expecting to feel the sizzling bullets of his assailant's weapon, but instead he got laughter.

"Blood, you slow than a mothafucka! If I was a crab, or one of the Mexicans, I would have floored you already!" Big Head threw his head back laughing.

"Well, nigga you're not!" Fat Travon shot back, annoyed.

"What chu doing out here this early anyway, fool?" he switched subjects, seeing his homeboy was on one. "What does it look like? The early bird catches the worm. I'm tryna get it." He replied like he should have known, serving a butch smoker two dime rocks. The exchange was so smooth that it looked like the two of them were just smacking each other five.

"I ain't mad at chu, Blood, but chu do know this the big homie's shit, right?" Big Head asked, knowing damn well Travon knew who corner he was hustling on; all the homies from the hood knew that Booby was running Gangsta's operation now.

"Man, fuck Booby!" Fat Travon spat angrily. "Blood might be y'all niggaz daddy but he ain't mine!"

"So what chu saying, my nigga?" he frowned up.

"What I'm saying is, Booby can eat a bowl of hot dicks and you can, too!" He stepped into the little nigga'z face, drawing his .32 pistol.

"That's how you feel?" Big Head mad dogged him, wanting to fire on his ass. He was so close he could smell the leftover liver and onions on his breath.

"Yeah, nigga, that's how I feel!" Fat Travon spat, his finger curling around the trigger of the small pistol. "Now run and tell your daddy that?" his head bopped from side to side as he talked that shit.

Big Head was pissed off; he clenched his jaws so tight that you could see the veins pulsating in his neck. He cursed himself for forgetting his strap at home, because if he hadn't he would have left fat boy belly up and leaking where he stood.

"Alright, my nigga," Big Head rode off on his Beach Cruiser.

"Yeah, that's what I thought, pussy! Kick rocks!" Fat Travon flexed, feeling himself. He harped up some phlegm and spat it on the curb, watching the little nigga'z back as he rode off down the street.

Meanwhile

Pavielle and Gouch were in the front yard of their grandmother's house throwing hands. Gouch took two solid punches to the chest from his baby brother. The blows stung like hell but he ignored the pain and moved in for some get back. He set Pavielle up throwing weak jabs, which he easily swatted away. He then countered with two solid punches to his sibling's rib cage and a hard right into his gut. Pavielle staggered back, wincing in pain from the devastating combination. The well placed punches nearly dropped him but he quickly re-established his equilibrium. Panting out of breath, but refusing to lose to his big brother, he tucked his chin to his chest and balled his fists as tight as he could.

"You done had enough, nigga, huh?" Gouch asked.

"Fuck that shit, Blood! You're gone come up outta my mothafucking Dickie's!"

Both of the brothers were exhausted from going from the shoulders with each other, but neither of them was going to throw in the towel any time soon. They were both stubborn, so their squabbling usually ended with both of them strewn out on the lawn from exhaustion.

"I told you these are mine, Booby!"

"I'm not tryna hear that shit, nigga!"

"I was going easy on your ass 'cause you're my baby brother and shit. But now the kid gloves are off."

"Bring that shit then, homeboy!" Pavielle threw a few jabs but they fell a couple of inches short of reaching Gouch's chest.

"What the hell are y'all doing?" Vayda yelled out from the porch, holding the front door open. "Baby, why are you fighting your brother?"

"Fuck this nigga, baby!" Pavielle yelled back, trying to punch a hole through his oldest brother's chest. "Blood tryna gangsta my Dickie's."

"You mean your red Dickie shorts? I took them to the cleaners with the rest of your stuff."

Pavielle dropped his arms to his sides and turned around to face his woman, breathing heavily. "And when in the hell were you going to let me know this?"

"I told you yesterday that I was taking them to the dry cleaners, weed head." She pretended to take pulls of a blunt, her way off letting her boo know he smokes too much weed.

"See, I told your ass." Gouch smacked him in the back of his head. He swung back around throwing up his hands and the two started slap-boxing. A sharp whistle came from their left and the brothers' heads snapped around. Beyond the iron-gate they saw Big Head on his Beach Cruiser.

"Soowoo," he greeted them.

"Soowoo," Pavielle and Gouch retorted in unison, as they approached the black iron-gate breathing heavily.

"What it two, my young nigga?" Pavielle asked, resting his arms between the bars of the black iron-gate.

"Ain't shit, y'all know Fat Travon posted up by y'all way getting it, right?"

"Hell naw! Where he at?" Pavielle frowned.

"Shit, right there in front of Ace's mini-market." he informed the brothers.

"That fool knows that's my territory." Pavielle told Gouch over his shoulder. "He thinks just 'cause unc is on lock that he can post up out here? It doesn't work that way.

Unc's territory is under my jurisdiction now. I'm running this." He smacked his hand up against his chest.

"I tried to tell 'em but he wasn't tryna hear me," Big Head confessed, looking dead serious. "He said, and I quote, 'Booby can eat a bowl of hot dicks!'"

"Is that right?" Pavielle asked, raising an eyebrow. He couldn't believe Fat Travon would show his ass like that.

This nigga know I'ma 'bout that life, fuck wrong with Blood? He thought.

"Yep, he told me to eat a bowl of dicks, too." Big Head added. "I'm telling you big homie, if I would have had my banger, I would have bucked his fat ass down." He extended his hand and pulled an imaginary trigger, making gunshot sounds with his mouth. "Pop! Pop! Pop! Pop!"

"Would have served him right, disrespectful mothafucka," Gouch's face balled up.

"Aye, Gucci, I gotta see this nigga. Yo, Y.G," Pavielle addressed Big Head. "Post right here for a second, Blood. I'll be right back." He ran off into the house and came back out loading pool balls into a black dress sock, tying it up at the end. "Roll me to where blood at." He hopped on the handle bars of Big Head's Beach Cruiser, his legs dangling as they rode off. His face was balled up and his neck was on a swivel as they moved.

Gouch snatched up an old rusty pipe from off the curb and was stalking after his brother and their homeboy.

The Hood brothers were about to fuck a nigga up.

***

Fat Travon had just finished making a sell when he looked up the block and saw Big Head, Pavielle and Gouch approaching. He tensed up a little, realizing he had let his mouth write a check that his ass couldn't cash. But it was too late now, he had to soldier up and hold down the fort. Readying himself, he put on his game-face and tightened his grip around the .32 resting in his jacket's pocket. He took a deep breath and then blew hard.

Big Head's Beach Cruiser came to a stop in front of Fat Travon and Pavielle hopped of its handle bars. Holding the sock of pool balls behind his back, he approached the stubby curb server wearing a hostile expression.

"What's up, fat boy? What chu doing out here?"

"Nothing," Fat Travon replied nonchalantly. "Tryna get this money."

"I ain't mad at chu, pimp. You can get your money.

You just can't get it over here," Pavielle informed him, tightening his grip on the sock of pool balls. "Gangsta's locked up and this here has been passed down to me. And the only niggaz that's living off the fat of my land is the ones that are getting money with me. Ya Griff me?" he spat on the sidewalk, wearing a scowl that dared Fat Travon to challenge his authority. "So you gone have to bounce." His eyebrows arched and his nose scrunched up, nostrils flaring.

Fat Travon's looked over Pavielle, Gouch and Big Head. They were all mad dogging him. Outnumbered, he felt like a lamb among a pride of lions.

"Or get bounced!" Gouch added, head bobbing from side to side. He was posted under the telephone pole with the rusty pipe resting over his shoulder like a baseball bat.

Big Head sat on his Beach Cruiser laughing at Fat Travon, taunting him. Pissed off, the stubby corner hustler drew his pistol. Before he could get off a shot, he felt something hard strike him dead smack in the face. A sharp pain shot through his face like a bolt of electricity. He grabbed his face with his meaty hands and dropped his weapon, right beside Gouch's rusty pipe.

Pavielle swung into action, assaulting Fat Travon with the sock of pool balls. He struck the beefy hustler's back, shoulders and head. He tried to make a run for it, but he tripped him up and he fumbled to the sidewalk, busting his mouth. The crack rocks spilled from his jacket's pocket onto the pavement. Two crack heads came out of nowhere snatching up the tiny pieces of poison. One of them scooped up his .32 and tucked it, running off with his partner.

Gouch caught up with his baby brother while Pavielle continued to beat Fat Travon with the sock of pool balls, kicking and stomping him the fuck out. Having grown tired of using the sock of pool balls, Pavielle flung it to the side and snatched an aluminum trash can from the curb. He motioned for his brother to get out of the way and then he slammed it on his victim's head, hard as a mothafucka.

"Uuuuh," Fat Travon moaned, eyelids flickering white.

"Stay the fuck off my blocks! Haa! Haa! Haa! Haa," Pavielle managed to say between breaths, his chest jumping up and down. He was winded from the beating he had laid down. He harped up some phlegm and spat it on Fat Travon's temple. The disgusting goo oozed over his eyelid, dripping to the ground.

Chapter Eight

The next day

Pavielle had gotten a phone call from a blocked number while Vayda was braiding his hair on the front porch. He started not to answer the call, but then he remembered that the plug was supposed to hit him up.

"What's bracking?" He said into his burn-out cell phone before taking a pull from his blunt, unleashing smoke. Afterwards, he tapped the L, dumping ashes on the step. The grayish black flakes floated and landed on the step below him.

"Is this Booby Loco?" A voice asked from the other end of the phone. It sounded like it had been chopped & screwed, like that music from Houston.

"Yeah, who is this?" His face balled up.

Ignoring Pavielle's question, the voice went on to give him the location and time he was to meet his charge.

Shortly thereafter, the phone was being hung up.

"Who was that?" Vayda asked, making a part down his head with a skinny comb.

"My destiny," Pavielle replied before taking another pull from the blunt, blowing smoke into the air.

That night

Eleven thirty rolled around and Pavielle and Gouch found themselves pulling up at the address the weird voice had given him. The address belonged to an old warehouse that used to manufacture Mattel toys.

Entering the mouth of the enormous warehouse, the headlights of Pavielle's Chevy Impala shined on the faces of Tango, Bullet and Black Jesus. The trio was posted outside of a white on white Rolls Royce Phantom. The luxury vehicle's headlights were shining behind them to provide light within the dark warehouse.

Pavielle left the headlights of his Chevy on and grabbed the duffle from the back seat. He jumped out of his ride with Gouch on his heels, approaching the drug lord and his company. Pavielle looked over the faces of the three men before him. He had no idea who the older Dominican gentleman was in the fancy suit and shades. But from the bulge near his left breast he knew he had to have been packing, which would make him Black Jesus' bodyguard. He couldn't have been the plug, because men of his caliber never carried a gun. They always had someone with them to hold them down.

Homeboy standing on the opposite side of the man in the wheelchair couldn't have been Black Jesus either. It was the shaved head, tattoos and gangster apparel that gave him away. His threads and appearance definitely wasn't one of a drug lord. From what Pavielle heard from Gangsta, his coke connect was a man who adored tailor made suits. He was into silks, suede and linens. You would never catch him in Dickie's and a Pro-Club.

The Spanish cat in the wheelchair had to be Black Jesus. He looked just like Gangsta had described him; a good looking, dark skinned Latino, with a Superman curl.

Pavielle thought if the drug lord hadn't chosen the dope game; the pretty mothafucka could have made his living as a supermodel.

"You must be Black Jesus?" Pavielle guessed right. Black Jesus cracked a grin but never answered. "I'm O.G Booby Loc, and this is my older brother, Gouch." He gave a slight nod to his big brother, who was standing beside him. "We're Gangsta's..." Pavielle's words died in his throat when Tango and Bullet drew down on him and his brother.

"Ain't this about a bitch?" Gouch's forehead wrinkled, looking to his little brother.

"My man," Pavielle scowled and addressed the wheelchair bound man. "What the fuck is this?"

"Place your guns on the ground, kick 'em over and take off your clothes." Black Jesus ordered.

"What?" Gouch snapped. "I'm not upping my strap, and I'm for damn sure not taking off my mothafucking clothes!" with that being said, Tango and Bullet the click! clacked! their weapons.

"Take. Off. Your. Mothafucking. Clothes," Black Jesus gritted, arching his eyebrows. "Now!"

"Go ahead and do as he said, Gucci," Pavielle told his brother as he removed his banger and dropped his duffle bag at his sneaker. Gouch blew hard but went along with his little brother's request. As the brothers placed their straps on the ground and kicked them over, Gouch stared at Black Jesus with a burning hatred. He swore to himself if he lived through whatever the drug lord had planned for him that he was going to put a bullet through his head and each one of his niggaz as well.

"Now your clothes, gentlemen," Black Jesus told them and steepled his hands in his lap. The brothers stripped down to their boxers. "And your boxers," Pavielle and Gouch exchanged glances and then they dropped their boxer briefs to the ground. They stood facing the Mexican drug lord, dicks and balls hanging. Black Jesus then motioned for them to do a 360 degree turn with his finger. They obliged.

"What's up with your man?" Gouch asked Pavielle as he turned around. "He's some type a fag or something?"

"No, I am not some type of fag." Black Jesus answered, overhearing the eldest of the Hood brothers.

"You don't get to play in this game as long as I have without taking precautions. Besides, I don't know you two from a can of paint. For all I know, you could have been wearing wires."

"Fair enough," Pavielle retorted. "Now can we put our clothes back on?"

Black Jesus gave them the go ahead and they put their clothes back on. He then had Tango kick their guns back over to them. The weapons went spiraling in circles en route to their owners, bumping up against their sneakers.

"Now," Black Jesus began. "It's our turn." He flashed a smile.

Tango and Bullet stripped naked while Pavielle and Gouch held their heats on them. They spun around slowly to let the brothers see that they were not wearing any wires. They then got dressed and stripped Black Jesus down to his nakedness. They took the drug lord under his arms, lifted him from his wheelchair and spun him around so that the brothers could see that he wasn't wearing a wire either. They then got him dressed and sat him back down in his wheelchair.

"My apologies," Black Jesus told the brothers as he buttoned up his shirt. "But I enjoy my freedom. One man's humiliation is a small price to pay for it; no hard feelings, huh?"

"No hard feelings." Pavielle agreed. "Like you said, you have to take precautions."

"And your brother?" Black Jesus asked Pavielle, but kept his eyes on Gouch.

"No hard feelings." Gouch reluctantly agreed. "Now can we get down to business?

A sharp whistle from Black Jesus brought forth the humming of an engine and the crunching of gravel. Next, came the tail lights of a U-Haul truck backing its way inside of the warehouse. The large vehicle stopped beside the connect and his people. Its driver side door opened and a man in a Dickie's uniform and cap jumped down. Black Jesus motioned the Hood brothers over and they came right away.

"Your drugs are inside of here, thirty kilos as agreed upon." He knocked on the steel shutter. The driver of the U-Haul tossed Pavielle the keys and he snatched them out of the air.

"I'll take that." Tango took the duffle bag from him and slid the strap over his shoulder.

"So that's it?" Pavielle asked.

"This will be the last time you see me and drugs in the same place together." Black Jesus told him. "From now on you will go through Tango." He placed a hand on his bodyguard's shoulder. Playing bodyguard for him was more so a front for the Dominican man. His main job was making sure that his boss's shipment got to and from its destination. As well as taking in to account that the clientele got what they asked for once a deal was brokered.

Pavielle was given a burn-out cell phone with one number in it. He was to use it whenever he was ready to re-up and then discard it. He would be given a new cell each time he was done with the old one. After he was given these specific instructions, he stashed the burn-out cellular in his pocket. He and Gouch climbed into the U-Haul and made their departure.

It was on now.

Chapter Nine

Pavielle had assembled an All-star dream team. The seven man crew hustled all day every day. Twenty-four hours a day, seven days a week. From sun up to sun down the crew was at it, pulling in every dollar that they could.

Pavielle's crew was bringing in so much paper that he was running out of safes and stashes to put it in. Business was good and everybody was happy. The dream team was hood rich and loving it.

Black Jesus had taken a chance on Pavielle and it had paid off. The young kingpin was making him a lot of money. When the damu would come and cop he would bring bags of money so large that it looked like he was going to do laundry. As time progressed the Arturos and the Hoods grew closer. Black Jesus and Pavielle's relationship had become like his and Gangsta's. The two were business associates as well as good friends. They hung out when ever their hectic schedules would allow it.

Pavielle was lying in bed asleep, when he was awoken by a combination of delicious aromas escaping from the confines of the kitchen. His nose alerted his empty belly to the scrumptious morning breakfast awaiting them. His belly growled at being teased and he licked his chops. Sitting up in bed, the young kingpin yawned and stretched. He looked over to Vayda and found her fast asleep. He smiled, kissed her on the forehead and threw the covers from over his person. He pulled a red homemade stocking cap down over his corn rows, slipped on some red basketball shorts, and slid his feet into some red corduroy house shoes. He then headed into the bathroom, where he washed his face and brushed his teeth. After giving himself a once over in the bathroom mirror, he made a beeline for the bedroom door.

***

G-momma had just pulled a pan of biscuits from the oven and placed it on top of the stove. She turned the fire off a sizzling skillet of bacon and laid all twelve strips on a plate covered by three paper-towels to absorb the grease. On the kitchen counter was the rest of the morning breakfast: scrambled eggs, pancakes, grits, hash browns and sausages. There were also glass pitchers of milk, orange juice and apple juice.

Crossing the threshold into the kitchen, Pavielle found Gouch with his face buried into a plate of food. Pulling his head up from his plate to suck his fingers, Gouch gave his baby brother a nod of acknowledgement. Pavielle chuckled and shook his head at the sight of his big brother. He looked like a baby with all of those grits and eggs around his mouth.

"What's cooking, good looking?" Pavielle asked G-momma as he wrapped his arms around her and pecked her on her mole spotted cheek. She was taking a sip of orange juice when he had crept behind her.

"It's all on the counter, Booby," She smiled, taking another sip of orange juice.

"Mmmmm," Pavielle said, looking over the feast his grandmother had prepared, rubbing his hands together hungrily. "Smells good, looks good," He told her, popping a strip of crisp bacon into his mouth. "Momma, I'll tell ya, if I was just a lil' younger I'd have to go ahead and wife it up."

"Oh, stop it, I bet you tell that to all of the girls," G-momma said, acting smitten, batting her eyes.

"Only the ones I fall in love with," Pavielle capped, popping the other half of bacon into his mouth.

"You better stop it now, before Vay come out here." she laughed.

"Good morning, family!" Vayda said, crossing the threshold into the kitchen. She playfully smacked Gouch upside his head and he looked up at her like she had lost her mind.

"Good morning, Vay," G-momma replied, fixing a plate.

"Good morning, momma," Vayda pecked her man's grandmother on the cheek as she received the plate of food from her. "Thank you." She said in a very upbeat voice.

"Oh, so your man don't get none of them kisses?" Pavielle asked, pretending to be jealous.

"Oh, my man gets all of that and then some," She told her boo before they locked lips.

"Aye, man, don't chu bee me and momma eating over here?" Gouch said, mouth full of food.

"Oh, leave them alone," G-momma said, looking at the two lovebirds. "Can't you see that they're in love? Me and your grandfather use to be just like that. We could never get enough of each other."

"Yeah, well, it makes me sick." Gouch replied with a mouth full. He glanced over to the lovebirds and found Vayda giving him the finger. He gave it back to her.

"Gucci, what have I told you about talking with a mouth full? You know better than that."

"My bad, momma," Gucci said, before washing his food down with an ice cold glass of milk."

"You should try to find yourself a nice clean girl like your brother." G-momma told him.

"I had a clean one last night, momma, but I dirtied her up." He retorted, eating scrambled eggs. G-momma couldn't help but to laugh and shake her head.

"Gucci, you're something else." She told him.

Vayda took a seat at the kitchen table and started in on her plate. Pavielle approached Gucci eating a biscuit; he stood over his big brother as he munched. When Gouch looked up and found his baby brother over him, he already knew what time it was.

"Move; it's too early to be playing, man." He told him, wiping away his milk mustache.

Pavielle chewed the last of the biscuit up and smacked the crumbs from his hands. He continued to stand over Gouch, staring down at the top of his head.

"Booby, sit down," G-momma told her youngest grandson. "It is way too early. Go ahead now. Sit." She motioned him to his seat, but he ignored her.

"Nigga, you touch me and I'ma put my foot in yo' ass." Gouch told him seriously.

"Gucci!" G-momma brows furrowed and she stomped her foot. "Watch your mouth."

"Yeah, Gucci, you heard momma, boy," Pavielle said, cracking his knuckles. "Watch your mouth!" his hand was a blur when he swung it, smacking Gouch upside his head so hard that it jerked violently. Gouch hopped to his feet and they tussled for a minute. Before long, the big brother had the little brother in a headlock and was twisting his knuckles into the top of his head.

"Aaaaaah!" Pavielle said in pain, feeling Gouch's knuckles turning the top of his scalp raw.

"Gucci, stop now, you're hurting your brother." G-momma told him, rising to her feet.

"Don't worry, momma, I got this fool." Pavielle said, trying to lift Gouch up off his feet. Veins bulged up his neck and forehead, as he struggled with lifting his sibling off the floor.

"Gucci, y'all heard y'all momma, stop now!" Vayda finally spoke up.

Gouch released Pavielle. The brothers stood facing each other, panting out of breath. Suddenly, Pavielle smacked Gouch upside the head again and bolted for the front door, laughing all of the way. Pissed off, the oldest of the Hood brothers charged after his baby brother.

Pavielle made it onto the porch and slammed the door in his brother's face. Gouch stood behind the black iron screen-door shouting threats. Pavielle gave his sibling the finger and made his way down the steps, chuckling. Reaching the pavement, he lit up a Newport and took a pull. He fanned out the match and when he looked up he saw Avenue across the street. The former singer turned junkie was dancing and singing. Every so often someone would cross his path and toss coins into the fedora at his feet. Pavielle watched him for a while before calling him over.

"Yo, Avenue," Pavielle called out and waved him over. Avenue stuffed the coins and the few crumbled dollars from the fedora into his pocket. He smacked the hat onto his crown and came running across the street in a hurry. He was excited. Nine times out of ten when Pavielle called for him he had a few dollars he could make.

"What's up, young blood?" Avenue asked, meeting Pavielle at the black iron-gate.

"You tryna make some money?" he asked.

"Hell yeah, I'm tryna make some money! What chu got for me, black man?" he rubbed his hands together greedily, licking his dry, cracked lips.

"Nah, I mean, some real money, not no five or ten dollars. I was thinking about putting you down with the team."

"For real?" Avenue raised his eyebrows, not believing his ears. "Oh, I'm down like four flats." He gave him a pound.

"There's a catch, though," Pavielle told him.

"What's that?" he inquired, wondering what the catch could possibly be.

"You've gotta get cleaned up, pimp. That's the only way I'm a put chu down." He paused and waited for a disheartened expression but he never got one. "You still fucking with me?"

"Hell yeah, I'm no fool. Let's get this money." Avenue gave him another pound.

"Alright then, man, I'ma give you like a week to smoke 'til you choke. But after that, it's rehab, baby."

"I can dig it. And thanks, man. Thanks for blessing me with the opportunity."

"Don't even worry about it O.G. Here," Pavielle reached into his sock; from the bulge in it you'd think he was hiding an ankle monitor for house arrest. He withdrew a bankroll of one hundred dollar bills, peeled off a bill and handed it to him.

"Damn, all of this is for me?" Avenue asked, holding the bill up with both hands as he looked it over. A smile stretched across his face, showcasing the rotten teeth in his mouth. He was as happy as a fag with a bag full of dicks having that much of money in his possession.

"Yeah, man, just do me a favor before you run off and spend that."

"Anything, my man," Avenue replied, stuffing the $100 dollar bill into his pocket. The mothafucka couldn't stop smiling, thinking about all the crack that Benjamin Franklin was going to buy him.

"Wax my baby for me," Pavielle pointed over his shoulder to the black Mercedes Benz 600 parked in the driveway, sitting on chrome 22 inch rims. "I just got her a couple of weeks ago and I haven't had the time to get her washed."

"Damn, that's you?" Avenue whistled at the sight of the luxury car. "She's beautiful. I'm a hook you up, my guy, I'm a detail her and everything."

"Sho' ya right," he smiled and gave him a pound.

"Everything you need is already in the trunk. You can get the keys and the vacuum from my girl. Go ahead and knock on the door."

"Alright then, let me go and get to work." Avenue said, coming through the gate.

Pavielle wasn't tripping off giving Avenue a hundred dollars to wax and detail his whip. It wasn't just because a hundred dollars wasn't shit to him. It was because the money was going to come right back around into his pocket anyway. Just as soon as Avenue finished waxing and detailing his car, he was going to go right over on 27th and cop his fix from Big Head. Pavielle was smart like that; he always thought two steps ahead of the rest.

"What set chu from, Cuz?" A voice rang from the right, putting emphasis on the word '*Cuz*'. The word sent chills up Pavielle's spine. Anytime he heard it he knew it was time for some drama. Some drama he wasn't quite prepared for, seeing as how he had left his strap in the house under his mattress. He cursed himself and was expecting to get gunned down after being caught slipping. If this was to be his last stand then so be it, but he wasn't going out like a coward. He blew the nicotine from his lungs, flicked the cancer stick and put on his game-face. Balling his fists, he turned around to where the voice came and met the smile of an old friend, O.G Bully. Pavielle smiled back and ran out of the yard like a kid after an ice cream truck.

"My gangsta is on his shit!" Bully said, embracing his little homie.

"All day, O.G," Pavielle responded, breaking their embrace. He took a step back to get a good look at his big homie. Besides the forty or so pounds of muscle he had packed on and the salt & pepper stubble of his chin and shaved head, Bully still looked the same as he did before he went in. "Damn, Blood, you done got big than a mothafucka, what chu you benching?"

"About two-fifty," Bully told him, flexing his 20 inch arms. "These are the only guns Binem will let me walk around with without locking my black ass up again."

"Is that right?" Pavielle asked. "So when they let chu out?

"Shit, like three days ago."

"Why didn't you call me, Blood? I would have taken you shopping and shit; gotchu some pussy."

"Had to get settled in and shit. Make a couple of phone calls. Go see my P.O. You know how it is when a

nigga first get out of the pen."

Pavielle nodded his head in agreement. He had never been to the pen, but he had plenty of homeboys who had. So he knew the program when first touching down. "Where you holed up at?"

"With Thangz and her grand momma over on 35th and Jefferson."

"You still fucking with Thangz, huh?"

"What chu mean, Blood? That's my girl."

Bully and Thangz had hooked up about two years before he went to prison. It was the perfect marriage, he was slinging for Gangsta and she was crack's latest victim. One night Thangz had tried to get him to get high with her. He'd turned her down several times but eventually his curiosity got the best of him and he decided to give it a try. From there on he'd gotten hooked and there was no turning back. He seemingly lost everything overnight. Broke and unable to support his habit, Bully picked up his gun and linked back up with his first love, jacking. He was robbing everything moving, even his own homeboys. Niggaz wanted to take his head, but it was Gangsta's influence that stayed them.

One particular night, Bully got it in his head to rob an Uber driver. It was Thangz job to distract him on one side, while he approached from the other with his gun. Everything had seemed to be going as planned until the driver swung around with a snub-nose .38, instead of a handful of cash. He shot Bully in the gut and sent him sailing back into the street. Bully took the wrap for him and his lady and winded up doing a nickel for armed robbery.

"My bad, my nigga, you got them chips we sent chu, right?" he took in Bully's gear. He was in a Platinum Fubu Jersey, Jordache Jeans and scuffed British Knights.

"Yeah, but after a couple of nights at the mo' with Thangz, a few bottles, and some weed, you know all of that shit gone." He chuckled and gave Pavielle pound.

Bully was full of shit; he saved every nickel that was put on his books. He had planned on using that money to cop himself some work and strong arming someone's block when he came home. At forty-six years old, he still had that goon mentality. He was going to get it how he lived, like he always had, right there in The Bottoms.

"I ain't tripping, though, it was well spent. My girl set

a nigga straight. If you know what I mean." He nudged Pavielle. Pavielle reached into his sock, pulled out the bankroll of bills and handed it to his big homie.

"Good looking, my nigga, I really appreciate this." Bully gave his little homie a pound before shoving the bankroll into his pocket. "Listen, you know I'm not really one to be having a brother feeding me. I'd like to get mine like a man, on my own two, you Griff me? I was hoping that chu put a nigga down with the team."

"What chu talking about, G?" Pavielle asked, playing dumb.

"Come on now, this O.G. I always keep my ear to the streets. Your name is hot up in them pens. Everybody knows about O.G Booby Loco; niggaz say you're the black Scarface."

Pavielle shot Bully a funny look and patted his chest down for a wire. Bully laughed and shook his head. "Fuck you wearing a wire or something?" he asked. "I don't know nothing about nothing, homeboy."

"Man, it ain't never like that this way. I'd off myself before I turned snitch," Bully told him. "All a nigga tryna do is eat, that's all. And I'm a do that regardless of whether you put a nigga on or not. I just thought since we're peoples I'd come to you first."

"Right, are you hungry?"

"Hell yeah, you know Thangz can't cook to save her life."

"Come on," Pavielle motioned for him to follow. "Momma just finished cooking a big ass breakfast and shit. You can fix yourself a plate and we can finish chopping it up."

"Two sho'," Bully replied following Pavielle through the gate.

Hours later

"Man, the O.G homie is really a booty bandit?" Gouch asked Bully. The two of them were sitting at the kitchen table inside the trap house on the corner of 28th and Compton Avenue.

"Hell yeah, that nigga running around Folsom fucking with them queens and shit." Bully shook his head. "Saying he ain't gay 'cause he's not the one taking it in the ass."

"Blood, a fag is a fag," Gouch declared. "I don't care if a nigga is catching or pitching."

"That's what I said, but when I was locked up a lotta niggaz on the yard thought they weren't gay 'cause they weren't the ones getting fucked."

"What up with O.G Birdman?" Gouch asked. "You run across him in there?"

Bully nodded his head. "I bumped into Birdman when I was in San Quentin. And let me tell you, the Birdman is as crazy as bird shit now. They were given out them flu shots up there and wasn't none of us fucking with it. But this mothafucka went and got one. Now, at first shit was all good, Blood was the model prisoner and shit. But as soon as them folks pushed that old bullshit into his veins, Birdman went coo coo for Coco Puffs. Fool ate three of his own pigeons, stripped butt naked, and ran through the mess hall slashing niggaz across the face." he swung around an imaginary shank, "I mean, this nigga was giving it to everybody; Mexicans, white boys, Asian mothafuckaz, C.Os, even some of the homies got cut. It took six of them C.Os to restrain the nigga."

"Damn," Gouch said, shaking his head.

"They whooped Birdman's ass for four days and four nights. And all that shit did was made blood even more brazy." Bully claimed.

"What happened after that?" Gouch asked as he sat up in his chair. "Shit, last I heard before I left he was in solitary confinement. He wouldn't eat none of the prison food they were trying to give 'em. He had acquired a taste for his own piss and shit." Gouch's face soured and his jaws swelled as if he was going to vomit. "Yep, they had him evaluated and the state declared him insane. Now he's at one of them asylums for the criminally insane."

"Man, O.G, if Birdman would have never stuck up that pet-store for that bird food that shit would have never happened to him." Gouch shook his head; he hated to hear about his big homie's misfortune.

"Nah, if he would have never gotten caught that shit would have never happened to him," Bully corrected his little homie. "But what are you going to do, my nigga?" he shrugged his shoulders. "This is God's plan." A sharp whistle came from Bully's right; he looked over his shoulder and found Pavielle tossing him a Saran Wrapped kilo of coke from the doorway. He caught the kilo and balanced it on his hand to measure its weight. He then took a look at it; it was stamped with the image of a Black Jesus Christ.

"Black Jesus, huh?" Bully said, staring at the holy image. "My little homies done graduated to the big leagues. I'm proud of y'all niggaz, Blood." He looked from Gouch to Pavielle.

"That's right there, my friend, is a key of the purest coke to ever touch the twenties; The Bottoms period." Pavielle stated proudly, eating a 35 cent bag of Flaming Hot

Cheetos. "Ain't no cut on that blonde haired, blue eyed bitch either."

"You ain't gotta tell me, this is the same Spanish mothafucka your uncle was copping his work from." Bully told him.

"Peep game," Pavielle began. "Cook that bitch up and break her down into twenties. That's how we're going to rock with that. Smokers start bitching about why they can't get dimes or nickels, then you send their asses over to the crabs 'cause from what I hear the work they got over there is doo doo. Bully," Pavielle leaned in closer to his big homie, placing his hand on his shoulder. "That monkey isn't still riding your back is it?"

"Ah, nah, I've been clean since I've been down," Bully proclaimed. "Five years now."

"You ever get…," Pavielle looked his big homie dead in his eyes. "that itch?"

"Nah, not even a little bit." Bully spoke with confidence.

"Yeah, but what about your girl, Blood? You know she's still on the pipe."

"Yeah, but what the fuck does that have to do with me?" Bully said, glaring at him. He didn't play that shit about his girl, anybody could get it around her.

"You know, recovering alcoholics stay away from loved ones that still indulge in the bottle," Pavielle told him. "So I would think with you being a recovering addict and all, you'd wanna stay as far away from users and crack as you can. I'm not knocking how a nigga eat and shit. I'm just saying, Blood."

"Listen, man, this is O.G," Bully told him, pounding the blood gang sign to his heart. "I got this, trust me."

Pavielle nodded his head. "Alright, O.G, no disrespect, but you should know that if you fuck up, I'll do you just like I'll do any other fool; big homie or not."

"I wouldn't have it any other way," he told him. "But like I told you, 'I got this'."

"Alright, follow me to the back." Pavielle motioned for Bully to follow him. He gave him a quick tour of the small three bedroom house and showed him the weapons he had stashed around the place in case any jackers kicked in the door.

***

Pavielle flipped on a light-switch and gave life to the mother of all shitty bathrooms. The once eggshell white walls and tiled floor were so filthy that they appeared to be gray. The commode was grimy and the bowl was clogged. The bathtub was just as filthy, only it was filled with a clear liquid.

Bully's nose wrinkled at the wretched stench coming from the shit-water inhabiting the commode. Pavielle was unfazed though, he had grown use to the foul odor and the disgusting bathroom. It was the second bathroom of the house and it was kept this way to keep mothafuckaz from using it. Pavielle had a damn good reason as to why. "What the fuck is that, old bathwater?" Bully asked, referring to the clear liquid occupying the tub.

"Nah, battery acid, pimp," Pavielle answered him. "What's the first thing the boys do before they raid?"

"Shit, cut the water off."

"Right, and why? So a nigga can't flush his shit." He answered his own question. "If the boys should happen to run up in this bitch, you grab whatever product you have left and dump it off in here. It should dissolve in a minute or so."

"Youz a smart mothafucka, Booby."

Pavielle nodded his head, agreeing with his big homie. He was use to people giving him compliments like that. He had always been street smart and book smart.

"At the end of your shift you'll report to Gouch. He'll swing by here every night after shop is closed, so have that scratch ready. I'll break you off at the end of the week; that's every Friday; seven hundred dollars. You do right. You handle your business. And I'll promote your ass. You'll move up to a bigger slice of the pie, bool?"

"Yeah, I can work this shit." Bully nodded and gave Pavielle a pound.

Chapter Ten

Nightmare sat on the living room couch before his "50 inch flat-screen, watching *The Boondocks* on cartoon network. He had the remote control in one hand while his other hand was shoved down the front of his Levi's, like he was Al Bundy or some shit. He was laughing his ass off at Riley Freeman's crazy antics when he heard his pit bull, Karma, barking. He pressed the mute button and silenced the flat-screen. He then snatched his chrome and his gold Desert Eagle .44 from the coffee table and ascended on the front door with caution. He wasn't sure who was at the door so he approached it from the side. There had been many incidents where an enemy would knock on a rival's door, wait for him to answer, and then open fire. The gangsta crip had lost three homies to that war strategy and he wasn't about to become a statistic.

"Who is it?" he asked over Karma's barking, expecting slugs to shred the front door, but they never came. Instead a voice responded.

"It's Supacrip and Nike, Cuz, open up!" a voice boomed from the opposite side of the door. Recognizing it, Nightmare tucked both of his head bussas in his waistband. He then undid the locks on the door and pulled it open. He stood to the side to allow Nike and Supacrip inside. The blue rags greeted their big homie as they crossed the threshold.

"Where my son at?" Nightmare asked as he chained and locked the door.

"Who? Taco? Cuz still in the trap," Supacrip told him as he rummaged through the refrigerator. He produced two chocolate pudding cups; he kept one for himself and tossed the other to Nike. Right after, he retrieved two spoons from the kitchen drawer. "You know my nigga stay tryna run a check up." He tossed Nike one of the spoons and hopped up on the counter.

"Like father like son. Lil' Cuz is all about a dollar. I should have named him Lil' Nightmare." Nightmare said, thinking of how hard his little homeboy hustled. "Y'all get them snaps to Reboc?" he asked, flicking the dirt from underneath his fingernails.

"Yeah, I had my lil' broad drop off that paper and some clothes to him." Nike told him. "You know I'm not stepping foot in The Jungle, too many Oh lahs for me."

"True that, but where them snaps at?"Nightmare inquired. With that question posed, Nike sat two duffle bags on the table and slid them before his big cousin.

"I know my goon tired of being up in there." Supacrip shook his head. He and that nigga Reboc were like brothers and shit. They'd been running the streets together since middle school. "What's it been? Two or three months now? He's living in a homemade prison."

"If that nigga suffering, it's his own mothafucking fault," Nightmare replied. He frowned when he only saw two bags on the table. He hadn't notice that was all his cousin had brought into the house when he first let him in. His eyes looked from the duffle bags to his relative. Nike shrugged like he didn't know what was up, but that was a lie. He just didn't want to be the bearer of bad news, but he was going to be in that position anyway. *This shit looking wayyy light, I normally see more duffle bags than this.* Thinking nothing of it, the gangsta crip opened up the duffle bags, continuing the badgering of Reboc. "He shot all them people on that live ass block. It ain't no telling who all seen his dumb ass. Supa, hand me that money-counter from under the sink." He told the young rider and torturer.

Supacrip reached underneath the sink and withdrew the machine. He sat it out in front of Nightmare and leaned his husky body against the kitchen counter, folding his arms across his broad chest.

"He told me and Nike that he's positive that nobody I.D'd him." Supacrip put him in the know.

"Still can't be too sure, so I'ma have Cuz lay low for like, another month before I see about getting him." Nightmare claimed, removing stacks of money from the duffle bags. Seeing this, Supacrip and Nike exchanged glances knowing that the inevitable was coming. They took deep breaths and shook their heads.

"That's smart."

Nightmare dumped the few stacks that were inside of the bag out on the table and disappointment crossed his face. Scrunching up his nose, he massaged his chin and shifted his eyes up at Nike who just shrugged. Next, he took a deep breath and opened up the second duffle bag, peering inside. There was even less loot in the last bag. He dumped out the contents of this bag and sat back in his chair, looking between his niggaz. Right after, he started running the bands through the money-counter. Once he figured out the math, he scribbled the digits on a small notepad and outlined it. He then tossed the ink pen and the note pad on the table.

"Yo, soooooo, uh," he scratched his temple wearing a dumbfounded expression, thinking on it for a moment before continuing, "This is all we pulled in? The homies got they issue?"

Nightmare and the other two leaders of the crips were part of a narcotics trafficking ring called The Three Headed Monster. If you hustled in their neighborhood you were either working for them, or they were the ones supplying you. Because if they weren't you'd find yourself with a bullet in your skull, lying in a six foot plot. The three headed monster was the governing body of the Eastside Crips, nothing went down without their say so. There was no one man above the collective, and one member's word couldn't override the others.

Nike slid his hands down his face and blew hard, cheeks puffing out. "Yeah, they got theirs. They weren't too thrilled about theirs either."

"Ok," Nightmare took a deep breath, eyebrows arching. "Help me understand what the fuck is going on here. 'Cause we use to pull in ten times this much, one of y'all niggaz pull my coattail, hip me to some shit. 'Cause this shit right here," he held his hand out at the stacks of money scattered on the table top, "this is unacceptable."

Nike polished off the chocolate pudding cup and tossed it into the trashcan. "For one, this work this new plug is hitting y'all with is trash, and for two, we got competition, competition that's sitting on some shit that's way better than what we got."

"Who?" Nightmare's forehead wrinkled, wondering who his relative was talking about.

"Booby Loco, the slob nigga from twinks; Gangsta's nephew."

"Yeah, I know who the nigga is. I use to go to 28th street School with him," Nightmare told him. He was sitting at the table now and homeboy had his undivided

attention. "Fuck he gotta do with this?"

"Cuz is the man over there now since Gangsta got locked up. Smoker fool told me they're pushing a product that's better than ours."

"So that's why our sugar has turned into shit, huh?" Nightmare tugged on his chin hairs as he stared aimlessly across the room. "I bet that's where all of our custies migrated to."

"No doubt," Nike nodded. "That work them niggaz got pulling in fiends like the Black Hole."

"You've been knowing this shit, and you just now pulling my coat?" Nightmare clenched his jaws and balled his fists tightly. He looked like he wanted to punch Nike dead in his mothafucking mouth.

"Fuck I care? Their business wasn't effecting our operation…until now." Nike stated. What neither of them knew was that although Booby was pushing the same work as his uncle, he wasn't as heavy on the bacon soda, so the crackheads were fucking with him tough. This was because his product was the purest that they'd ever gotten their hands on.

"Did you know about this shit, Cuz?" Nightmare looked to Supacrip.

"I've heard talks, but like Nike said, Loc, I wasn't worried about it 'cause it wasn't effecting our thang, feel me?" Nightmare thought on it for a minute and nodded his head. Rising from the table, he drew a butchers' knife from the block on the counter and rounded the table, twisting the tip of the blade into his nail. Nike's eyes shot to their corners and he kept a close watch on him. Although they shared the same bloodline, the little buff nigga knew that his cousin wouldn't think twice about jamming the knife into his eye socket and popping his eyeball out of his fucking skull. The nigga was known for being an unpredictable psychopath. Friend or foe could fall victim to his wrath.

"This nigga fucking up our paper, taking food outta our families' mouths and shit," Nightmare began picking the scum out of his nails with the knife, "You thinking what I'm thinking, Supa?"

"Yeah, we dead our competition," Supacrip spoke with a dead serious expression. He had his eyes locked on the knife in his big homie's hand, seeing a gleam sweep up the length of it. See, he had an idea what he planned to do with it and he was glad he wasn't in Nike's shoes. All he could do was shake his head.

Poor bastard, he thought to himself, feeling sorry for Nike.

"Right, and find ourselves a new connect. I've been chopping it up with this nigga Nate and he said he may be able to plug me in with his peoples. Now, I don't know how good his peoples shit is, but it's gotta be better than what we've got." Nightmare circled the table for the second time with Nike's eyes glued to him. The boy was nervous and it was showing. Beads of sweat had started to form upon his forehead, running down his face. He swallowed the golf ball size lump in his throat and wiped the sweat from his brow with the back of his hand.

"What about this nigga Omid?" Supacrip asked.

"He's not going to take too kindly to being cut off. You know how these Arab mothafuckaz are, especially these eastern Muslims. Those boys are itching to die for a cause.

I heard they're promised something like seventy-two

virgins and their own paradise in the next life. So they ain't gotta problem with blowing themselves up just to take out an enemy. And this towel-head has an army of these mothafuckaz in pocket, us cutting him loose is sure to start up a war."

Nightmare nodded his head in agreement, Supacrip was right. "You let me worry about that fat greasy bastard. I'll take care of him." Nike's hands had a slight tremor, but Nightmare hadn't noticed. He was too focused on picking the scum from out of his fingernails and chopping it up with Supacrip.

"What about the powers that be, do we hip them to this?" Supacrip inquired.

"Nah, not yet, Cuz," Nightmare answered, placing a firm grip on his little cousin's shoulder. He looked like he was about to wet his 501s. "This shit stays between us three right, Cuzzo?" he said to Nike, his mouth right by his ear. With the knife in his hand and him being so close, Nike was petrified. Sweat had begun beading on his forehead. He didn't know what to expect next.

"Unh huh," Nike nodded his head, shutting his eyelids for a moment and swallowing his spit.

"Good. As for that nigga Booby…he's a dead man!" With a grunt, he slammed the Butcher's knife into the kitchen table, startling Nike and lodging it in place.

Chapter Eleven

Pavielle and Vayda enjoyed a fun filled night at the Santa Monica pier. They made their rounds visiting the Ferris wheel, the bumper cars, The Wave Jumper, The Air Lift, The Pirate Ship, The Sea Dragon, The West Coaster, The Pacific Plunge, etc. They even played a few ticket games. Pavielle had won Vayda a huge stuffed Teddy Bear with a big red bowtie. He had beat out four other people playing that game where you shoot a clown's mouth full of H20 with a black water pistol until the balloon above its head inflates and explodes.

The lovebirds made silly faces as they took photos inside of a picture booth. They purchased cartoon drawings of themselves and some of those fake tattoos. Pavielle ate a caramel apple while Vayda pigged out on cotton candy. They ate corndogs and shared an XL 7up and Hawaiian punch mixed fountain drink. After a few games on the arcades, Pavielle thought they should take a walk out on the beach. He was a helpless romantic underneath his macho exterior, so he knew how women ate that kind of corny stuff up.

Pavielle and Vayda walked the shores barefoot, hand and hand, carrying their own shoes. "Wow!" Vayda said, looking up into the sky at the twinkling stars sprinkled throughout the entire galaxy. The sight was definitely one to be admired.

"Yeah, wow," Pavielle repeated, marveling the stars above alongside his boo as they traveled along the sandy beach. "Being so caught up in the streets I never took the time to appreciate things in life."

"Things like what?"

"Sunsets, walks on the beach…love," he smiled, locking eyes with the love of his life.

"Love?"

He nodded, yes. "Love can make you feel special. Love can make you feel lucky. Love can make a broke nigga feel like he's the richest man in the world. Shit, when you think about it, love is like a drug. And you can spend the rest of your life high." Dropping his shoes, he stopped and turned to Vayda, taking her hand into his own. He stared into her eyes romantically. "Love is right here, babe. It's between you and I. You are my drug, Vayda." Her eyes instantly welled up with tears and before she knew it they were jetting down her face. She bit down on her bottom lip and sniffled. At that moment in time she felt blessed to have met the man of her dreams and she hoped that they stayed together forever.

It was just the two of them against the world.

"As you are mine," She replied with the utmost sincerity. He pulled his red bandana from his right back pocket and dabbed away her tears with it, as she continued to cry and sniffle. After stashing his bandana into his back pocket, he took her hands into his and kissed them. The two kindred souls stared deep into one another's eyes. There was a moment of silence as their hearts shared a magnetic attraction. The electrical charges the two love muscles generated drew them in closer to one another. The separate entities yearned to be together as one.

Holding on to one of his lover's hands, Pavielle got down on one knee and reached into his leather jacket, producing a flawless, 18k platinum engagement ring. A square cut pink diamond sat at the center of the ring, while the rest of the band was littered with smaller white diamonds. Vayda gasped at the sight of the ring, throwing a manicured hand over her mouth. Tears rolled down her cheeks, causing her eyeliner to run. She squeezed her eyelids shut for a time and peeled them back open, praying to God Almighty that she wasn't having a dream. She wasn't having one so it had to be true that a fairytale had been spun right before her very eyes. Vayda made an ugly face and broke down sobbing, tears flooding her cheeks. Taking her time, she swiped away her tears; she felt her heart rate speed up watching her man down on his knee, about to propose.

"Vayda Denise Perry," Pavielle's eyes became glassy and serious. "Will you marry me?" he popped the question, hoping that she'd say yes and make him the happiest man in the world.

"Oh, yes, Pavy. I'll marry you." She shouted, jumping up and down and fanning her tearing eyes. Pavielle slid the engagement ring onto his future wife's finger and they embraced, sharing a passionate kiss.

"There's something I've gotta tell you." Vayda told him after pulling away from their lip lock.

"What's up?" wonderment came across his face. Without saying so much as a word, she took both of his hands and placed them on her stomach, smiling from ear to ear. "You mean?" His eyes lit up with life and his mouth hung open.

"Unh huh," She nodded rapidly, giving him that breath taking smile of hers.

Excited, he grabbed her up under her arms and lifted her up off her feet. He spun her around in circles. They stared into one another's eyes laughing and smiling happily.

"Set me down, bae, I'm starting to get dizzy." She told him and he obliged her. He kissed her and hugged her again, rocking back and forth with her in his embrace. He cupped her face and kissed her hard, deep and passionately. Staring into her pretty greenish blue eyes again, he kissed her one more time on her lips.

"How far along are you?" he asked her.

"Three months." She smiled happily, holding up three fingers.

A voice began to sing *Unchained Melody* by The Righteous Brothers in sync with a violin playing the song's music notes. Hearing the beautiful song, Pavielle interlocked his fingers with Vayda's, both turning around in the direction of the singing. At the ends of their line of vision they found a clean cut Avenue in a sharp ass mustard green suit and a pair of black Mauri gators that were so shiny that you could see your reflection in them. Standing beside him was a young African American violinist playing the hell out of his instrument. The former Mesmerizers' crooner held a brimmed hat to his torso as he sung his heart out. Luther Vandross, Stevie Wonder, Al Green, Curtis Mayfield, Marvin Gaye; old Avenue could blow with the best of them and hold his own. That was for damn sure.

"Oh, baby, this is so beautiful," Vayda said, holding her hands over her mouth as tears streamed down her face.

"May I have this dance?" Pavielle asked, bending forward and holding out his hand. Vayda took it and rested her head against his chest as they slow danced, moving to the rhythm of the music. Vayda shut her eyelids and wished this moment would never end. She hoped this wasn't all a dream, but if it was she didn't want to wake up…ever.

Pavielle looked over to Avenue and gave him a thumb up, Avenue smiled and continued to croon.

The young kingpin's marriage proposal went beautifully.

An hour later

Pavielle and Vayda played the backseat of his Mercedes Benz as Avenue pushed the wheel back home.

The redbone couldn't take her eyes off of her engagement ring; it was as if she was watching her future unfold in the diamonds before her. Every so often Pavielle would glance over at her and flash a smile. It felt good to see his lady so happy. Her happiness meant more to him than his own.

"Where do you wanna get married at?" Vayda asked her husband to be, leaning her head against his shoulder and hooking her arm within his.

"I don't know," he shrugged. "Where ever you want is good with me. Planning weddings, baby showers, and

proms, all of that stuff is for females."

"Is that so? Well, what's for men then, Mr. Know It All?"

"Fixing shit, making money, proposing and making babies." Pavielle stated proudly with a smile, rubbing her stomach and envisioning the life growing inside of her.

"Babies, huh? Well, I want lots and lots of babies."

"Is that, right? How many?"

"Four."

"That's it?" Pavielle asked as if four babies weren't many to have. "I was thinking eight."

"Well, it's settled then, we'll have eight kids. Then I want a big house with a white picket fence, a Labrador retriever and a family station wagon. I want a great big old family, and I want us to do all of the corny things you see families do on television and in the movies, what about you, babe?"

"Whatever you want, boo, it's your world. I'm just happy to be in it." He curled his finger under her chin and kissed her on the lips and forehead.

"Oooh, I can't wait to get home and tell momma," Vayda shrieked like high school girls do when discussing their crush.

Avenue pulled the Mercedes Benz into G-momma's driveway. He executed its engine, slid out from behind the wheel, and opened the back passenger door. Standing to the side, he waited until Vayda and Pavielle had gotten out and then shut the door behind them. He then withdrew a cloth from his suit and began wiping the down the foreign whip.

Vayda ran into the house screaming to G-momma that she was getting married. Pavielle couldn't help but smile as he made his way up the stepswhere Gouch sat on the porch flipping through a family photo album, taking pulls of a Newport. The oldest Hood brother made eye contact with his baby brother as he approached.

"Say it ain't so, Booby, say it ain't so. Tell me your not really finna wife that ho?" he song then busted up laughing.

"Watch your mouth, nigga," Pavielle frowned and pointed a threatening finger. "That's the future Mrs. Hood right there."

"Tisk, tisk, tisk, haven't you learned anything being my baby brother? You don't go and buy the cow when you can get the milk for free." He shook his head in disappointment.

"Gucci, what the fuck are you talking about?" Pavielle asked, not having a clue of what his big brother was getting at.

Gouch shook his head again and went back to flipping through the photo album. "2+2 ass nigga," he said under his breath.

"Put some bass in your voice, fool. I can hardly hear you."

"You're simple, mothafucka! Simple!"

"Man, fuck you!"

He looked him over and said, "You're not my type."

"Anyway, what chu looking at?" Pavielle asked, looking over Gouch's shoulder.

"Photo album, what's it look like?" he turned the page to a mangled, creased picture of an African American couple. The man in the photograph held an uncanny resemblance to Gouch. But whereas Gouch was tall and lanky, the man was tall and ripped with muscles. The woman beside him had more of his little brother's features: narrow face, bowed lips and slanted eyes. The couple was dressed in black jeans and black leather jackets, sky blue turtlenecks underneath them. The girlfriend wore her hair in afro puffs while the boyfriend wore his in six neat cornrows. He clutched an M-16 in one hand and an AR-15 in the other while his better half gripped a 12 gauge shotgun.

"That's moms and pops, huh?" Pavielle leaned in closer to the picture, smiling.

"Yeah, that's them," Gouch smiled, admiring the old photo. "Man, momma was fine. I wonder if she was considered a dime piece back in the day."

"Yeah, momma was fine." Pavielle cosigned with a smile. His mother really was a beautiful woman. "But look at pops, Blood. He was buff than a mothafucka. Nigga look just like you and shit."

"Blood do kinda look like me." Gouch agreed, nodding his head. "And your ass look just like momma. All you need are some afro puffs."

He laughed.

"Gucci, tell me again how they were killed." Pavielle sat down across from him on the balcony.

"Goddamn, man, I told you the story a hundred times already." Gouch complained, blowing smoke out into the air.

"I know, Blood, but tell me again...please." He pleaded with his hands together as if he was praying. As gangsta as his ass was he looked like a little kid in that moment.

"Alright," Gouch gave in, taking another pull of his cigarette. He blew the smoke from his nostrils and flicked what was left of the cancer stick, sending embers flying. "This is the last time I'm telling you this shit, so listen up." He closed the photo album and Pavielle sat up ready to listen, looking like a kid at school during story time. "Okay..."

Gouch went on to tell the story.

Flashback

Robin Vines and Joshua Hood were once the members of the defunct Black Panther Party. The party dissolved in 1982, but the couple along with a handful of comrades decided to carry on the legacy through a new movement of their own called The B.P.P aka The Black Power Posse. The posse needed funding, so they went to the drug dealers of the community asking for donations. They figured since the hustlers had been peddling poison in the community for so many years that it was about time that they contributed to helping the environment that they had helped to destroy. After being told by the dealers to go fuck themselves, the posse picked up ski-masks and guns and took to robbing them. Every dime the posse jacked went towards funding the movement, which helped the poor families within the poverty stricken neighborhoods. The B.P.P was literally stealing from the rich and giving to the poor. So the neighborhood dubbed them as the names of their two leaders suggested, Robbin' Hood, as in Robin Vines and Joshua Hood.

Robbin' Hood left a bad taste in the local hustlers' mouths, so the dealers came together. They combined their moneys and put out a hefty bounty on the organization; $400,000 dollars for the capture of Robbin' Hood, dead or alive. The very communities that Robbin' Hood had sworn to protect and serve turned against them. In just a few weeks six members of the movement was gunned down like rabid dogs in the streets. The city ran red with blood and chaos.

The streets had gotten so hot that Robin and Joshua had disbanded their organization and sent their two boys to stay with Robin's parents. The couple became fugitives and went into hiding. While on their hiatus they put their heads together and came up with a plan. They were going to rob the biggest heroin dealer in Southern California, Anthony Philmore a.k.a Cadillac Tony. Tony had over a dozen dope houses scattered throughout Los Angeles, with each one grossing a minimum of $50,000 dollars a day. The man was a low key multimillionaire. Robin and Joshua were going to take their proceeds from the lick and move out to Oakland, where they'd start their organization over from scratch.

The couple were going to hit the Pueblo Del Rio housing projects, where Tony did his weekly count of the proceeds he made trafficking heroin. Every Sunday at twelve midnight a carrier would drop off Tony's take from the dope houses. Robin and Joshua were going to force their way into the apartment behind the carrier, take the bag of money and raid the spot for whatever cash that may be stashed inside. The couple did their homework and rehearsed their plan a thousand times. They had it down pact, so the lick was going to be a piece of cake. But before the couple could put their plan into effect something tragic happened, Robin was gunned down at a phone booth, while placing a call to her parents to check on the boys. Joshua was devastated once he caught wind of his wife's murder. He was hurting, but he was still going to carry out the mission they had planned. He knew that's what she'd want to happen. Once Robin was buried he decided to finish what they'd started.

Sunday night came bringing a storm and hard rain along with it. So when Joshua slipped on his black army fatigues and cap, he draped a poncho over it. He dressed his face in war-paint and loaded his weaponry into a black gym-bag. On his way out of the house, he stopped at the framed portrait of his family sitting on top of the television. He picked the portrait up, kissed it and placed it back down before heading out of the door.

Joshua laid on the roof of a house across the street of the housing projects. Scoped, infra-red rifle in hand, he picked off the armed guards on the roof of Cadillac Tony's complex one by one, dropping their mothafucking asses. The armed guards collapsed like a house of cards upon impact of the silenced weapon's bullets. Next, Joshua drew his hunting knife and started in on the armed guards patrolling the grounds around the heroin dealer's complex. He moved so quick that he was nothing more than a blur before the guards' eyes. Before the guards could pull the triggers of their weapons, their throats were slit and they were toppling like dominos. Joshua dragged their bodies to the tenants' trash bens and dumped them. Once they were taken care of, he hid himself within the shadows and waited for the carrier to arrive. Seeing the carrier about to knock on the nigga he'd came to rob apartment's door, he sprung into action and pressed his banger into his kidney. The carrier's eyes doubled and he stiffened, eyes shooting to their corners. A gloved hand pressed down over his mouth and a deep, raspy voice whispered into his ear. The breath of the voice was so hot it made the carrier's ear moisten and the hair stood up on the back of his neck from fear.

"You should know before you knock on that door, that if you alert who's ever in there to my presence. I'm going to kill you first. Got it?" the frightened carrier nodded yes. "Carry on."

The carrier knocked on the door in a specific pattern. A moment later, five locks were undone and the door was pulled open. Before him stood a burly Nigerian man, with high cheekbones and a head as wide as a Rottweiler. He wore a button-down shirt, slacks and Ostrich skin shoes. The holster strapped under his arm held a large caliber pistol. The hulking man was Cadillac Tony's bodyguard, Bruno.

Bruno locked eyes with the carrier and could tell something was wrong. He was sweating profusely and he seemed tense.

"Are you going to let me in before I catch the flu, big man?" The carrier asked, trying to keep his cool. The giant narrowed his eyelids at the man and looked down at his feet. Noticing a second pair of boots behind his, he scowled and went to draw his burner. And that's when all hell broke loose.

Joshua shot the carrier in his back and kicked him in his ass. He stumbled towards Bruno with the bag of money and the ebony brute swatted him like a fly. The stumbling carrier created a diversion just long enough for the ghetto avenger to open fire on the hulking bodyguard. Bruno jerked violently as an entourage of bullets ripped through his chest. Joshua grabbed him by his tie and pulled him close to use him as a human shield; he had peeped Cadillac Tony going for his gun when the first shots went off. Cadillac Tony had rose to his feet from the kitchen table, where he was eating fried Jumbo shrimp and French fries, pulling his burner. He tried to draw a bead on his intruder, but couldn't see him over Bruno's wide back.

Bruno's three hundred and fifty pound limp body proved to be too much for Joshua to maneuver and he found himself pinned between the Nigerian and the carpet. He struggled to free himself from under the dead man, but his efforts were futile. Cadillac Tony ran upon his dead bodyguard's corpse and leveled his gun at his back, finger fucking the trigger. He fired round after round into the obese corpse hoping the bullets would come out the other end and strike their intended target. But he had no such luck, the fatty tissues of the dead man's hefty frame had stopped the bullets midway through.

Click!

Click!

Click!

Tony's burner went empty as he pulled its trigger. He quickly discarded it and went to cease the .38 in his ankle holster. That's when the back of Bruno's skull exploded as three rounds found their escape. The bullets slammed into Tony's belly and he fell over onto the floor, wincing. His face held an expression of confusion and agony, as he lay on his back staring up at the ceiling. The lower half of his shirt was completely red.

Joshua freed himself from beneath Bruno and removed the .38 stashed in his victim's ankle holster. He stuffed the small pistol into his waistband and pulled the heroin peddler upon his hands and knees. He then dog-walked that ass into the bedroom where he was sure he'd find a safe full of money. Joshua parted the clothes hanging on the bar inside of the closet and discovered a black stainless steel safe built into the wall. He smiled to himself thinking of all the cash that might be inside: one million, two million, three million, maybe. He pressed his steel to the side of Tony's dome and told him to open the safe. To which he replied, "Fuck you, old bitch ass nigga!"

"Run that by me one more time, boss," Joshua frowned and listened closely. His victim spat blood on the carpet and repeated himself, "What chu hard of hearing, mothafucka? I said..." that was as far as he got before his brains were blown all over the safe in the wall. Joshua lowered his smoking weapon and abandoned Tony's body in the bedroom, casually making his way inside of the living room. He could hear police car sirens wailing in the distance, so he had to work quickly. He grabbed the bag of money the carrier had dropped and refilled it with the $100 dollar bills that were scattered over the floor. Once he was sure he had every bill accounted for. When he looked up he locked eyes with the carrier, he was wearing a gold police shield around his neck. His left hand was holding his bleeding gut while his right held a standard police issued handgun. He was glistening with sweat and by the look on his face his wound was showing him no mercy.

"D.E.A, asshole," He exclaimed breathing hard as a bitch. "Drop your weapon!" Joshua stood there like a dear in headlights. He was taken by surprise; he couldn't believe the carrier was an undercover law enforcer. Of all the rotten luck he had. "You hear me, cock sucker?! I said, 'Drop your weapon, both of them!'" he demanded.

The police had just arrived on the scene. Joshua could hear their wailing sirens right outside the door. Surrendering, he discarded his gun and tossed the .38 stashed in his waistband. The agent ordered him to his knees, with his hands behind his head. He complied and the agent approached him with caution. The ghetto avenger eye-fucked his captor as he ascended on him, gun at the ready. He waited until he was three feet away and unsheathed his knife where was strapped on his leg. He smacked the burner from the agent's grasp and grabbed him by the collar of his shirt, poking his ass up with his knife, blood squirting everywhere. Joshua stared the dying man in his eyes. Behind a mask of pure hatred, he said, "Sell out ass, mothafucka." The agent's pupils dilated and he released his last breath.

Joshua let the agent's limp body crash to the surface and spat on his corpse, totally disrespecting it. As he rose to his feet the police came flooding into the apartment, guns drawn. They looked from Joshua to the dead agent at his feet and then back again. Hate and disgust was etched upon each one of their faces. Joshua shut his eyelids and tilted his head back, taking a deep breath, inhaling the fragrance. It was the perfume scent of his wife, Robin. She had come to take him away to a place where they could be together forever. He smiled. The police took it as a smack in the face since he had just murdered one of their own, and they fired upon him with extreme prejudice.

Pop! Pop! Pop! Bloc! Bloc! Splocka! Splocka! Boc! Boc! Poc! Poc! Poc!

The cops pumped one hundred and fifty rounds from their weapons, and about a hundred of them ripped through Joshua's body. He danced on his feet for a time before his hole-filled body went crashing to the carpet, creating a pool of blood beneath its self. His face held a slight grin as a lone tear slid down his cheek. Robin's ghostly image leaned over his strewn body and planted a gentle kiss upon his lips. With that, he expelled his final breath and left this life for a better one.

Present

"Man, pops went out like a G behind his." Pavielle stated proudly. "When I go out, I wanna go out just like he did; for a cause I believe in; for something I was trying to achieve, you Griff me?" Gouch nodded yes. "We're going to take the crack game to the next level, where all of my niggaz seeing a million or better. It won't be no hating or none of that shit; everybody gone eat."

"That's what I'm talking about." Gouch gave him a pound.

"I'ma take it in, Blood. I'm tired than a bitch." He patted his brother on the shoulder and headed into the house, shutting the door behind him.

Chapter Twelve

A month later

Bully was slumped down in the butter soft leather seat of a silver X5, sitting on twenty two inch chrome rims. He gangster leaned as he pushed the big body down Crenshaw Blvd. Gripping the steering wheel with a jeweled hand, he banked a right onto MLK blvd, nodding his head to Kanye West's *You can't tell me nothing.* He had just left the Baldwin Hills Shopping Plaza. He had purchased a new fit from Men's Land, a fresh pair of kicks from the Foot Locker, and a bottle of cologne. As of now, he was headed back to the house to take a shower and get dressed for Pavielle's birthday party. He couldn't wait for the young kingpin to see the gift he had gotten him. He had made it himself.

It had been a few months since Pavielle had put him down and he was seeing some paper. All the bad bitches were checking for him now. Bully was getting more money and pussy than he knew what to do with, but he never let it go to his head. He humbled himself and kept it one hundred how a real gangster is supposed to. He made sure he took care of Thangz. Even though she was a hard up Junkie, she was one of the few besides Gangsta that held him down during his stretch. He had a lot of love for the busty crackhead, and that hadn't changed, even when he found out she was turning tricks to support her habit while he was locked up. Though Thangz was a walking corpse she was still his boo. So he had to stick with her and help her put the pieces of her life back together.

That night

Detectives Arsenegger and Ortiz sat parked outside of G-momma's house watching as the guests arrived for Pavielle's birthday party. They snapped pictures with hopes of matching the unfamiliar faces with the names they had back at the precinct.

"Pavielle Hood and Black Jesus Arturo in bed together; why aren't I surprised?" Arsenegger asked no one particular from behind the wheel. He was looking over Ortiz's shoulder as he snapped pictures of the party guests.

"Gangsta put up the line between the two of them, no doubt," Ortiz claimed, snapping the pictures. "Guy gets popped and sets his nephew right up; who else more fit to helm the throne than a direct blood relative, with the business sense and know how?"

"Keeping it in the family," Arsenegger added.

"O.G Booby Loco's the man now. He and his crew have The Bottoms sewn up with weight. The little guys can't even eat. You either get on their payroll, or get filled with some hot shit." He continued snapping the pictures.

"I'm going to personally see to it that that piece of shit and all of his associates are behind the zippers of body bags. And you can take that to the bank and cash it." Arsenegger said, looking at the guests entering G-momma's house.

The blue eyed devil was going to make good on his word...or die trying.

***

Pavielle's party was as live as the Mayweather Vs De La Hoya fight. G-momma, Vayda and Gouch had put together one hell of a shindig for their loved one's 26th birthday. All of the homies and a few Bloods from other sets came out to show Booby Loco from Outlaws 20s some love. Black Jesus, Bullet and Tango even turned out. There were bottles of Ace of Spades, Rose, and Chardonnay on ice. G-momma and Vayda had prepared a feast fit for a king and his knights. And since it was Pavielle's birthday, she allowed the guests to put cigarette and weed smoke in the air.

"Alright, Booby, Y'all done wore momma out; I'm finna head to bed now." G-momma pecked her youngest grandson and caressed the side of his face lovingly. "I love you."

"I love you too, momma." Pavielle said from the arm of the couch, drinking from the bottle of Rose.

"I love you too, momma." Neck Bone snickered, mocking his homeboy from the floor, where he was slow dancing with a sexy brown skinned number from BSP. Pavielle gave his goofy ass homeboy the finger. Neck Bone laughed and cuffed his dance partner's fat, juicy ass.

"Aye, fool, help momma to her room." Pavielle told Gouch, who was at the opposite end of the couch. He had a hood rat from around the way on his lap and a clear plastic cup of Hennessy in his hand. He was faded than a mothafucka, eyes red webbed and hooded.

"Aye, raise up, I gotta help my momma to bed." Gouch told homegirl occupying his lap. Once she got up, he hooked his arm with G-momma's and led her toward her bedroom. "Right this way, madam." He said in an English accent. He cracked a smile and she returned it.

"Oh, y'all outta here?" Pavielle asked Black Jesus, seeing Tango push him towards the door with Bullet bringing up the rear.

"Yeah, I'm calling it a night," Black Jesus replied, giving him a pound. "I have a lot of business to attend to in the morning. Being a business man yourself, I'm sure you understand."

Pavielle nodded his head. "Alright fam, hit me when you make it home so I'll know you got in safe." he patted the pretty boy drug lord on the shoulder. He then gave Bullet a pound and a hug. "Alright, my nigga, take care of my boy." he told him before giving Tango a nod; the Dominican bodyguard returned the gesture. Although

Tango hadn't done anything to him personally, it was something about the old Spanish gangster that didn't quite sit right with him.

After seeing to it that Black Jesus and his entourage made it into their ride and off the block, Pavielle wandered around the house looking for the future Mrs. Hood.

"Yo, Ridah Man, you seen my old lady?" He stuck his head into the kitchen, where he saw his crimey pouring himself a drink as he chopped it up with a few of the homies and some females from Westside 20s.

"Yeah, she went to the back with that nigga Bully." Ridah Man answered, not thinking anything of it. Although his answer struck a chord in Pavielle and jealousy reared its ugly head, he took a long drink from his bottle and wiped his mouth with the back of his fist. Next, he burped and stormed into the corridor, where the bedrooms lined the hall.

***

"You think Booby will like it?" Bully asked Vayda as she looked over the painting he had did as a gift for Pavielle; the two of them were in the bedroom where all of the gifts were.

Vayda seemed to be amazed by all of the talent that the muscle bound hoodlum possessed. At first she just figured him to be your typical gangbanging ass street nigga, but

145

now she felt that she had the O.G pegged all wrong. "Oh, he'll just love it," Vayda assured him. "This looks just like him and Gouch when they were little. You captured their parents well, too. Your painting looks so life like."

"Thanks. G-momma gave me a picture of them. It was kind of mangled, so I had to work with it. You think you can help me wrap it up?"

"Sure, I've got some wrapping paper leftover from earlier in the closet." She told him, handing over the painting and making a move for the closet.

***

Unbeknownst to Vayda and Bully, Pavielle was outside the bedroom door with his ear pressed up against it, listening in. Only he wasn't hearing the conversation they were having about the painting. Nah, see the combination of weed and alcohol had him so delusional that he actually believed he was hearing the moans of his lover as she was being pleasured. The young kingpin's face twisted into a mask of murder as he continued to listen to the sexual encounter his mental had conjured up. He snarled and gripped his bottle of Rose so tight that it cracked at the neck, traveling down the length of it. No longer able to tame his jealousy, Pavielle took a step back and kicked the door with all of his might.

Boom!

The door flew open, sending splinters of wood flying everywhere. Vayda and Bully were startled and confused, they didn't know what the fuck was going on. Pavielle came charging in with murder on his mind, he threw his bottle of Rose at Vayda's head and she evaded it. The bottle shattered into pieces against the wall. The alcohol that it contained ran down the wall and soaked into the carpet.

"You fucking this nigga at my party?" Pavielle roared with a pair of dangerous eyes. Before the redbone could plead her case, her face met the opened hand palm of her enraged lover. The smack was so vicious that it whipped her head around and echoed out into the hall, grasping all of the guests' attention. A frowning Bully could have sworn he saw sparks fly from her cheek.

Vayda hit the bed and rolled off onto the floor, holding her redden hand imprinted jaw and sobbing her eyes out, hot tears flooding her cheeks. Pavielle stared down at Vayda, chest rising and falling as he breathed heavily. He stayed focused on her, looking down at her like she'd lost her goddamn mind.

"Blood, what the fuck is your problem?" Bully's forehead wrinkled with lines. "We weren't in here doing nothing, we still got our…"

"Fuck you, nigga!" Pavielle barked on him, the spit flying from off his lips. In a flash his black .9mm was up and off of his waist. He shot his big homie's through his thigh, causing him to clench his teeth. The muscle head nigga dropped to his knees, clutching his thigh and making blood seep between his fingers.

"Aah, fuck! Sssssss!" Bully withered in agony, biting down on his bottom lip to fight back the fire burning in his thigh. He'd been gangbanging all of thirty three years and shot more enemies than he could count on both hands, but tonight he finally got a taste of his own medicine. *Hot lead!*

While Bully grimaced in pain, Pavielle pressed his head bussa into his forehead and applied pressure to the trigger, mad dogging him and biting down on his inner jaw. Gouch grabbed his baby brother by the wrist and threw his arm up, just as the gun went off. The bullet struck the ceiling and debris trickled down. Everyone crowding the hall and looking inside hollered. The sound of the weapon was unexpected and startled them.

"What the fuck is your problem, man?" Gouch snarled, snatching the .9mm from his grasp and shoving him into the wall. Right then, Pavielle came back to the present, blinking his eyes, looking like he'd suddenly been shaken up from his sleep. His head snapped to the doorway and he found his guests there, staring at him like a patient that had just escaped from an insane asylum. That's when the reality of what he had done hit him and he brought his hands down his face, taking a deep breath.

"We weren't in her fucking, Blood; on the set!" Bully swore between groans of pain. "Ahhh! Sssss! Sssss! Shiiiet! I got too much love for you to play you like that, Booby. I was just showing her the gift I made you. She was going to help me wrap it." He looked to Gouch and threw his head toward the present. "Check it out."

Gouch picked the painting up from the floor and looked over it, cracking a grin at what he was seeing. "He ain't lying, bro. It's a painting of me, you, moms and pops." He turned the painting into Pavielle's direction. Staring at the painting, Pavielle felt like a real jack-ass for what he had did to Bully. All he could do was look at him withering in agony while clutching his bleeding thigh.

"Didn't you see we still had our clothes on when you busted in here?" Bully inquired, his face displaying all of the pain he was feeling. Pavielle nodded yes and helped his big homie up to his feet.

"Ridah Man, Neck Bone," Gouch called for his homeboys. "Y'all two niggaz take O.G up to general hospital, Blood." The homies retrieved Bully from Pavielle and left to do as they were instructed. "Alright, y'all the party is over, you don't have to go home but chu gotta get the fuck outta here!" He told the guests. With that said, all of the guests made their way back up front.

"Gucci," G-momma called out from her bed-

room. "Is everything alright out there?"

"Yes, momma, we're just out here cleaning up," Gouch spat the lie as soon as he brainstormed it. "Go back to sleep." He turned to his little brother, pointing his long, crooked finger in his face. "I should kick your black ass, nigga, gone and go check on your girl!" He ordered, throwing his head towards the door.

"I love you, Gucci," Pavielle proclaimed with a drunken slur.

Gouch blew hard and brought a hand down his face, massaging the bridge of his nose. He looked at his baby brother, grinned and shook his head. "I love you too, you stupid mothafucka. Come here," He opened his arms and Pavielle gave him a brotherly hug. The killer pecked his younger sibling on the cheek and ruffled his hair affectionately. "Gone and get your ass in there with your lady, man. I'ma make sure all of these mothafuckaz done cleared the house."

"Alright, Gucci, I'm sorry, man. I'm sorry," Pavielle slurred, his eyes filled with moisture and sadness. Gouch nodded his head and headed out of the door. "I love you, man!" he called out after his big brother as he disappeared into the hall. Crossing the threshold he took in all of the faces of the people who were looking at him crazy. "Fuck y'all looking at?" he mad dogged them. Some of them turned their heads while others allowed their eyes to linger on them before sighing and keeping it moving.

***

Vayda stood before the bathroom mirror sobbing, as she gave herself a once over. The left side of her face was swollen and bruised. Although the side of her face was sore and throbbing, she was more so hurt that Pavielle had the audacity to put his hands on her. She knew from her previous relationship that if a man put his hands on you once, more than likely history would repeat itself.

Pavielle stood in the doorway watching the love of his life weep, her pain tortured his soul. He couldn't believe he put his hands on her and he wished that he could go back in time and change everything. It was far too late though, because the damage was done.

Pavielle wished that somehow he could take her suffering away and bear the burden himself. Seeing his boo in her current state made him glassy eyed. He bowed his head and before he knew it the tears had came, dripping from the rims of his eyelids like droplets from a broken faucet. Taking a deep breath, he wiped his eyes with the back of his shirt's sleeve and sniffled. Afterwards, he cleared his throat and pulled himself together before approaching her.

He came from behind her planting soft kisses on her neck and collarbone. She shut her eyelids enjoying the feeling of his tantalizing touch, but wanting him to stop. She was confused. Her body was screaming *yes, yes, yes* but her mind was saying *Don't let this nigga touch you after what he did.* Although she tried to fight it she was finding herself falling weak. Vayda pleaded for Pavielle to stop, but her pleas became moans of pleasure, as he kept at it. He slid his hand down to her crotch, unzipped her jeans, and glided two fingers inside of her. She gasped as soon as his fingers pierce the opening of her treasure. Licking and sucking on her earlobe, he worked his fingers in and out of her warm, moist pussy.

"Ahhh! Ssssss! Mmmm," With her eyelids still shut, Vayda threw her head back, allowing underneath her chin to be exposed. Abruptly, she grabbed a hold of the back of his neck and propped her leg upon the commode, wanting his fingers deeper inside of her. She grinded on his hand looking like she was dancing provocatively, like those dread lock rocking broads at Jamaican clubs. Pavielle's fingers felt so good in her that she was too choked up to let out a moan. Her grip tightened around his neck and her knees buckled. Still, she continued to grind upon his hand like it was a dick. Sensing she was about to explode and spray the bathroom with her love nectar, Pavielle removed his fingers and turned her around to face him. He traced her lips with his glistening finger and then pierced them, allowing her to suck on it. She grabbed him by his wrist and stared into eyes, sucking on each one of his fingers. Her head movements looking like she was giving him a blow job. He mumbled something freaky under his breath, feeling his dick become engorged with the rush of his blood. His mushroom tip expanded and pulsated, dying to be inside of her tightness. The sound of her juicy mouth working his fingers had him bone hard. In a hurry, he stripped her naked, hoisted her around his waist and carried her into the bedroom. He laid her on her back and parted her legs, leaving him face to face with her fat, shaved pussy. That mothafucka was jumping like it had a heart and oozing with her clear, hot liquid.

Pavielle was a pro at sex; he had a tongue game that rivaled his dick game. And on some nights the two had a chance to compete for which was the best at what they respectively did. He went to work, nibbling and sucking on Vayda's clit. The Creole goddess raised her pelvis from the bed and brought herself closer to his mouth. He stared her dead in her eyes as he feasted upon that small flap of meat nestled between her southern lips; before he knew it she was walking the sheets and whining, asking him what he was doing to her body? He ignored her question and pinned her legs down to keep her still. About ten minutes later, Vayda unleashed a shrill of pleasure loud enough to disturb the deaf. That night she had four orgasms, coming harder than she had ever come in her entire life. Pavielle's sheets were so soaked that they had to sleep on the floor.

***

Pavielle awoke the next morning and discovered Vayda was gone. On the pillow beside him, where she was lying on the floor, was an envelope with his name on it. Frowning, he snatched it up and ripped it open hastily. He tilted the envelope over into his palm and the engagement ring he had purchased her slid out, along with a note. When he saw these items his heart skipped a beat and he feared the worse. Swallowing spit, he sat the engagement ring on the dresser and unfolded the note, his eyes quickly scanning over it. It simply read, *'We weren't meant to be in this life, but maybe we'll be destined to in the next'*. Glassy eyed, he reached over his head and picked up the Bic lighter on the dresser. He struck a flame and set the note a blaze, observing it withering and blackening at one end. He turned the burning note to the side, watching the fire devour its being. Once the flames began to work their way up near his fingers, he tossed the piece of paper into the waste basket. He watched the flames rise from the waste basket, as tears slicked his cheeks and a golden illumination shone on his face.

***

Pavielle sat in the La-Z-Boy Reclining chair in the den; chain smoking and singing along to R.Kelly's *When a*

Woman's fed up. The den was so foggy from smoke that he could barely be seen within it. He was wearing a stained wife beater, gray boxer briefs, which where stained yellow at the crotch and brown at the ass. He hadn't bathed in a while and was stinking something awful. His cornrows were frizzy and unkempt. His eyes were red webbed and there were black bags under them. And on top of all of that, he had grown a five o'clock shadow. He was a hot ass mess since his lady had left him.

Two weeks had passed and he had yet to hear from Vayda. He wanted so desperately to call her and beg her to come back, but the G in him wouldn't allow it. The way he saw it, pleading for a bitch to come back was for lames and simps. He had no intentions on giving in to that little voice in the back of his head. So for now, he was going to listen to heartbreak music, smoke, and drown his sorrows in hard liquor. Afterwards, he was going to fuck as many bitches as humanly possible until he finally got Vayda Denise Perry out of his system.

G-momma came into the den coughing and spraying Glad Air-freshener. "Booby, I don't know how many times I've told you and Gucci about smoking in this house. It's like the older y'all get the least you two listen to me. Y'all know better. Now put that out, I wanna talk to you." She turned off the stereo system, pulled up a chair beside her youngest grandson and sat down. Seeing that he was still taking pulls of the cigarette, she shot him a dirty look. Without protest, he mashed out the Newport in the ashtray, snuffing out its ember end. Next, he reached on the side of the La-Z-Boy and grabbed half a bottle of Jack Daniels. He screwed the cap off and just as he was about to take a drink, G-momma snatched the bottle from his hand causing lines to appear across his forehead.

"Ah, come on, momma!" Pavielle whined, throwing his arms in the air. He was irritated and wanted to be left alone to sulk and listen to his music.

"*Ah, come on, momma,* nothing!" She told him, screwing the cap back on the small bottle of Jack Daniels and then shoving it into her house coat's pocket. "I've been seeing you walking around her moping and smelling like God knows what for a week. That's not gonna get that girl back. You do want her back, don't you?" he shrugged his shoulders. "You can save that tough guy act for the streets, 'cause grand momma knows you better than anyone else. Better than yourself, even. Listen, Booby, if you want something bad enough you've got to get out there and get it. It's not going to come to you. And if you sit around waiting for it to come around to you, then somebody will come along and take it for themselves." She caught Pavielle looking away as if he wasn't trying to hear her, so she took him by the face and looked him in the eyes. Wetness accumulated in his eyes and his hurt came running down his cheeks. His reddened nostrils flared and he sniffled, breathing hard. His heart was aching and he wanted his woman like he wanted his next breath. It was just like his grandmother had figured. He wanted the love of his life back. "Remember this…anything in this world worth having is worth fighting for. I don't care if it's a promotion on your job, custody of your children, or the love of a good woman. If you want it, I mean, if you really want it, then you've got to get out there and fight for it. Trust me; you don't wanna wake up every day wondering what could have been if you only would have done something. Take advantage." They embraced and he sobbed into her bosom like he did when he was a little boy and had hurt himself. She kissed him on the cheek and held him a while longer, caressing his back trying to make him feel better. When she pulled away she grasped both of his hands and looked into his eyes. She told him to go out there and get his queen before taking her leave.

Pavielle journeyed back inside of his bedroom where he found a portrait of him and Vayda on his nightstand. Staring at the photo caused a smile to etch across his lips. A host of memories zapped through his mental, hitting him back to back. He knew in his heart that she was the one for him and he wanted her back in his life forever. He thought about what G-momma had said: *Anything in life worth having is worth fighting for.* Then he thought back to Vayda. *Was she worth fighting for?* Fucking right his baby was worth fighting for. She was worth killing for. She was worth dying for. She was worth living for. And he sure as hell was going to do whatever he had to do to get her back.

Pavielle called Vayda every twenty minutes. When she didn't answer he left messages. Once her voice mail filled up, he texted her. He then sent her countless messages through Facebook, Twitter, Instagram, Snapchat and email. He waited an hour, but still no word from his boo. So he decided to take it to the streets and hit up every hotel, shopping mall, grocery store, and restaurant she may be. He was going to start at all of her favorite hangouts and work his way down.

Pavielle took a quick shower, shaved, threw a stocking cap over his frizzy braids and got dressed. He hopped into his '96 Chevy Impala and hit the streets looking for his boo. He searched for his woman like the Terminator searched for Sarah Connor. He checked every spot he could think of but he came up with nothing.

Pavielle didn't get back home until 1:30 P.M that night. He lay in bed watching the ESPN sports channel, with

Damu snuggled under him. The dog could tell his master was depressed and he wanted to comfort him. This was the best way he knew how; men's best friend. G-momma had made her youngest grandson his favorite meal in hopes of cheering him up. Pavielle was too depressed to eat a single bite. So the fried catfish, cornbread, yellow rice, and broccoli went untouched. The only thing on his mind was Vayda. He wanted to be near her; to feel her body pressed against his; to run his fingers through her curly her; to kiss her full lips; to inhale her scent. It was like he had said the night at the pier when he had proposed, '*She was his drug*,' and he needed his fix.

After letting Damu loose inside of the patio, Pavielle rummaged through the few articles of clothing Vayda had left behind, trying to find one that still wore her scent. He came upon a beige satin bathrobe. Holding the robe to his nose, he closed his eyelids and inhaled deeply. Taking in her essence, he smiled and took another whiff.

"Damn, babe, a nigga missed you so much," he said just above a whisper. Using one hand to hold the robe to his nose, he used the other to unzip his Levi's and pull out his meat. He huffed and puffed as he jerked off, pulling and tugging on his dick. Tears rolling down his face, he uttered his lover's name over and over again as he neared his nut. "Vayda, Vayda, Vayyydaaaa, ahhh, Vayda, I'ma 'bout to…I'ma 'bout to cum, boo," His eyes rolled to the back of his head and his mouth stayed stuck open, making croaking noises. It was almost as if she was right there with him and he was fucking her up against the wall. He could have sworn that he heard her moans of passion and felt the grip of her pussy. Veins formed up his neck and became visible on his forehead, soon after he was shooting his load across the bedroom. Holding the robe down at his side, he continued to stoke his dick until he was empty. His entire form shuddered, feeling the aftershock of him busting a nut. Wiping his hands off on the robe, he then climbed into bed and balled up into a fetal position. Thoughts of his fiancé invaded his mind before the Sandman eventually arrived and carried him off to sleep.

***

Pavielle was awoken the next morning by the crowing of his Mexican neighbor's rooster. Slowly coming around, he felt a small hand reach inside of his jeans and take a hold of his morning wood. Instinctively, he went to reach for his .9mm on the nightstand. It was gone. *Fuck,* he thought and his head snapped over his shoulder. He found Vayda holding his own gun to his dick head, her finger curled around the trigger. Her eyelids were swollen and her eyes were pink and glassy. It was obvious to him that she'd been sobbing, probably ever since she'd left the house that night.

Pavielle swallowed the ball of nervousness in his throat and prayed that she didn't do what she had in mind.

"I love you, Pavy," She began, snorting snot back up her nose. Tears trickled from her eyes. "God knows I do, so my dumb ass is going to come back to you. But if you ever, ever put your mothafucking hands on me again, I'm going to blow your fucking dick off." she blinked and more tears jetted down her cheeks. "Do you understand me, nucca?" her voice cracked under her emotions, but she was dead ass serious. If he ever laid hands on her again, she was going to blow his dick off and empty a whole magazine in his chest, straight like that. Pavielle closed his eyelids and nodded in agreement.

Slowly, Vayda took the burner from her man's dick and sat it down beside her thigh. The Creole vixen broke down and sobbed uncontrollably. Pavielle put up his meat and

157

zipped his jeans back up. He then cupped her face and kissed her all over it, telling her how much he missed, loved, and needed her in his life.

"I'll never do anything to hurt chu ever again, ever. You hear me, baby? I love you too much to lose you, boo.

You're my queen. You're my queen and I'm your king." He kissed her on the lips and held her tightly as she sobbed into his chest. Tears ran down both their faces as they sat up wrapped in one another's arms. They then fell asleep hugged up with dry white tears staining their cheeks.

Love was a mothafucka.

Chapter Thirteen

Later that day

A black Mercedes Benz pulled up outside of Thangz Aunt's house. Avenue hopped out of the car and went around to the back passenger door. He pulled the door open and stood to the side as Pavielle made his exit. Stepping into full view the young kingpin saw Thangz coming out of the house with a big cardboard box, followed by Bully on crutches. Seeing what he had did to his big homie made Pavielle feel even worse than he did the night he had shot him.

Bully saw Paville headed his way and he called Thangz over. The busty crack fiend loaded the last box into the back of the U-Haul, closed the shutter, and ran right over to her man. Keeping his eyes on the young kingpin, Bully whispered something in his lady's ear and she looked over to where he was looking. She scowled at the man that had wounded her nigga then ducked off inside of the house to do as she was told. Pavielle saw the exchange and figured she was running off to retrieve his gun. And if that was so he couldn't blame him. He hadn't seen his big homie since the night he had shot him. He probably didn't know what to expect from the unannounced visit.

"What's up with it, O.G?" Pavielle gave him a pound.

"What's up with chu, damu?" Bully replied nonchalantly.

"Ain't shit, it's been a minute. Just thought I'd swing by and chop it up with my nigga," he told him. Looking over Bully's shoulder, he saw Thangz standing in the doorway, with her hand behind her back. She was holding her man's gun, no doubt.

Thangz was strapped and paranoid. She and Bully had been up smoking crack from dusk 'til dawn. The doctor had given the O.G some painkillers for his wound, but they weren't as effective as the crack rocks he scored from the Mexicans.

"I see your lady over there holding it down," he nodded to Thangz in the doorway, and Bully glanced over his shoulder. "I'm not mad at her though. My girl would be doing the same thing if the shoe was on the other foot." Pavielle cleared his throat with his fist to his mouth and continued. "Look, Bleed, I'm not really big on apologies, so…" he tossed him a bankroll of hundreds the size of a small roll of toilet paper. "Why don't we just let bygone be bygones, so we can get back to getting this money."

Thangz licked her chops from the doorway at the sight of all that money her man was just given. All she could think about was how much crack they could score with it.

Bully tossed the bankroll up and down in his palm as if it were a baseball. He paused for a minute as if he was thinking about something and then he tossed it back over into Pavielle. The young kingpin seemed to be taking aback by his big homie forking the money back over.

He thought for sure at the sight of a roll that thick he'd have no problem getting him back on the team but he was mistaken.

Thangz could have had a heart attack when she saw her man cough all of that money back up. A bankroll that size could have had them beaming up for at least the next couple of weeks.

Damn, she thought, *why my man gotta be so stupid?* She twisted her lips and stomped her foot, throwing a fit like a big ass baby.

"I'm good, pockets still fat," Bully patted the bulge in his pocket. "Besides, I'm leaving the hood. Don't you see that big ass U-Haul van in the driveway? I'm outta here."

Pavielle looked to the U-Haul and frowned when he saw the big ass moving van. He didn't know how in the hell he had missed it.

"Leave? With all of this money in the hood, fuck you tryna leave for?" Pavielle looked at his homeboy like he was crazy.

Bully took a deep breath and massaged his chin, trying to find the right words. "Have you ever seen a western where's two bad-ass gunslingers in town, and one tells the other, 'This town ain't big enough for the both of us?' Well, this hood ain't big enough for the both of us, and if I stay then one of us gotta die. The streets already talking, they waiting for me to off you. It's in my jacket: Original Gangsta killer. I'm known out here for putting in that work, niggaz know my resume. These fools aren't

going to let me walk these streets if I don't kill you. And if I do that it would break my best friend's heart, as well as my own. I can't do that to Gangsta. So I may as well save myself the embarrassment and shake the hood, you Griff me?"

Pavielle nodded his understanding. What Bully was doing was best for the both of them. He didn't know it but his little homie had a new found respect for him.

"Alright, Blood, but at least take these ends," he held up the bankroll.

"If it will make you feel better," Bully said, taking the bankroll and shoving it inside the pocket of his jacket. He then held out an arm to embrace Pavielle. The young kingpin stepped forward and they embraced in a gangsta hug.

"I love you, Blood, and I'm sorry about all of this shit," Pavielle spoke sincerely, breaking their embrace.His eyes held moisture. He was genuinely hurt that he'd let his jealousy get the best of him and placed a wedge between him and his homie. If only he could press rewind and take that bullet out of his homeboy's leg and put it back into his gun and his gun back on his hip. He would, no questions asked.

Damn, all this shit is my fault, Pavielle thought to himself and shook his head.

"I love you too, Duce Owe," Bully replied, heading towards the U-haul van, where Thangz was waiting behind the wheel. Pavielle stood on the curb and watched the van drive away until it disappeared into the florescent rays of the sun.

***

Avenue was laid back in the barber's chair with his eyelids shut. He was in Ms. Turner's Barber Shop on 22nd and Central. After dampening the ex-singer's facial hairs with a hot, wet towel, the slender Ms. Turner had began lathering his five o'clock shadow with shaving cream."I really appreciate chu blessing me with the job and all those fly ass threads, new school."Avenue told Pavielle, who was sitting in the barber's chair beside him. He was also getting prepped for a shave.

"Think nothing of it, old school. If we don't take care of our own, then who will?" he asked.

"I hear you, but what I mean to say is...Thank you. Thank you for helping me salvage what's left of my life. I really mean that." He said seriously.

"You wanna thank me? Thank me by knocking out this rehab program."

"Oh, no doubt, you got that, new school. It's the least I could do." Avenue responded. "I want chu to know that I'ma dedicate my life to this thing of ours," He tapped his fist to his chest. "And I'll die for this shit." he stated proudly.

Pavielle flashed a slight grin.

An hour later

Pavielle made his way out of Ms. Turner's Barber Shop eating a bag of Hot Cheetos. Avenue came out right behind him brushing down his fresh fade with a jeweled hand. His new hair style accompanied by his new gear made him look like a completely different man. In fact, if you were to lay eyes on him at this very moment, you would have never guessed that he had been smoking crack for the past thirty-five years. Looking to his right Avenue saw a beat up, old Monte Carlo with a missing headlight coasting up the block at five miles per hour. Avenue's street sense, much like a Spider Sense, kicked in and an alarm sounded off inside of his head, *danger, danger, danger.*

Suddenly a cell phone went off diverting Avenue's attention from the suspicious car on the creep. He looked to Pavielle who had drawn his cell phone from his hip. The young kingpin sucked the Cheeto residue from his fingers as he stared at the screen of his cell phone. "Fuck this nigga won't?" he frowned, seeing a name of a nigga that he didn't want to fuck with on the screen. "Oh." It dawned on him who it was that was hitting him up. He pressed *talk* and brought the cellular to his ear. "What's up with it?"

Avenue turned back around and saw the MC barreling their way. The back passenger window rolled down and the murderous scowl of a coldblooded killer came into view. He had a blue bandana tied around his head 2pac style. It was Supacrip. He stuck something out of the window long, black and deadly. It looked like it could clear a block of fifty niggaz.

"It's murrrdaaa!" Spit flew from Supacrip's big chapped lips as he chanted and held back the trigger of his automatic weapon. The assault rifle chattered, its flickering flames laying down pedestrians, shattering the windows of parked cars and the window of Ms. Turner's Barber Shop. Some of the patrons managed to take cover when the shooting started.But those who weren't as quick on their feet ended up lying on their backs in a pool of their own blood. The barber shop's walls and floor were splattered with their insides, pieces of their skulls, brain fragments and hair.

With lightning fast reflexes, Avenue freed his .357 Magnum from his waistband and swung it around, finger fucking its trigger. He let off four quick shots; two went wild and the other two married the back passenger door of the MC. Avenue continued to fire on the approaching hoopty. It wasn't long before he heard the sound that all street niggaz dreaded in a shootout.

Click!

Click!

The missile shaped bullets from Supacrip's assault rifle chewed up Avenue's face and chest, blowing chunks of bloody flesh out of his ass. He hastily stumbled backwards and fell over onto the sidewalk, resembling bloody hamburger meat. His life's blood ran off the curb and dripped down into the gutter.

The MC came to a screeching halt at the center of the block outside of Ms. Turner's Barber's Shop. Supacrip looked over the sidewalk at all of the bodies he had laid down for his main target, O.G Booby Loco.

"Cuz, did you get 'em? You get that nigga Booby?" Nike asked from behind the wheel of the hoopty.

"I'm not for sho, I laid a couple down though," Supacrip spoke honestly, still looking over the bodies on the sidewalk.

"Fuck, Cuz, I always gotta clean up yo' mothafucking mess!" Nike sucked his teeth and grabbed the mini M-16 assault rifle resting in the passenger seat. He swung open the driver side door and hopped out. Approaching the sidewalk, he could hear police sirens approaching in the distance.

"Hurry up, Cuz, one-time coming," Supacrip called out from the backseat.

Stepping upon the sidewalk, Nike fired rounds into the bodies of the pedestrians squirming about on the curb. Their blood splattered and specs of it clung to his pants legs. There was no way he was leaving any potential witnesses alive. He looked to his right and found Pavielle lying underneath Avenue. His eyes were staring out of their corners and his mouth was ajar. He was dead. Nike smiled wickedly and retreated back to the car. He slid in behind the wheel, threw it in drive and floored it away from the murder scene.

The next day

With the competition now eliminated, Nightmare moved to find a new cocaine connection and severe ties with Omid. As predicted things didn't go over too well with the big man; Omid was a notorious hothead who had to have it his way, or no way at all. So when Nightmare told him he was going to be taking his business elsewhere, he went ape shit on the phone and promised on his dead mother's soul to have every member of his family tree murdered.

Before Nightmare could get another word in edge wise, the dial tone was going off in his ear. The gangster crip knew he was a walking dead man; Omid had enough money and resources to wipe his entire hood off the map.

So he'd have to get to the Arabic drug lord before he got to him.

Nightmare had his little homeboys, Domino and Wacko, tail Omid for a week. During their investigation they learned that Omid didn't have a daily routine, but he did have three vices he couldn't live without: food, fine cigars, and black pussy. One of those three would be his downfall.

"Ah! Ah!" Omid shouted in sensual bliss. His eyelids fluttering as he balled the sheets up into his meaty fists. His wide, fat hairy ass was bent over in the do65ggystyle position. Pumping the twelve inch purple, see-through strap-on dildo in and out of his asshole was a curvaceous, busty, African American Dominatrix in a Cleopatra hairstyle wig and violet contact lenses. She was fucking the hefty easterner like a man would fuck his woman, and he was enjoying every minute of it.

A film of sweat had formed on Cleopatra wig's forehead, she wiped it away with the back of her hand, and continued to handle her business. She pushed and pulled the freakishly large fake cock from Omid's rectum, smacking his bare ass as she did so.

Smack! Smack!

"Uhhh, faster, baby! Faster!" Omid cried out, his face a mask of pleasure. "Ah, right there, here daddy comes…" he trailed off as he approached his orgasm. His penis stiffened and oozed with semen right before he collapsed onto the bed. Cleopatra wig collapsed right beside him, panting out of breath. He lied on the bed sucking his thumb, something he always did after sex. He then crawled over to the dominatrix, grabbed her by the strap-on penis, and began sucking on it, sloppily. As he deep throated the rubber cock, he stared her dead in her eyes. She grabbed him by the back of the head as he bobbed up and down her strap-on.

"Yeah, that's it, suck my dick, bitch," Cleopatra wig egged him on, sweat dripping off of her brow. She hissed like a snake and sucked her teeth, holding the back of his head as he slobbed up and down her artificial dick. "Deep throat this big mothafucka." She told him forcing his head further down the strap-on, causing him to gag and become teary eyed.

Although the dominatrix acted as if she was enjoying herself, she was actually very disgusted. But since she was getting paid top dollar for the sickening act being performed, she quickly pushed her judgmental thoughts to the back of her mental. Still, she couldn't get over the fact that the rich and powerful man before her was a closet homosexual. When he rolled up on the ho-stroll looking for some late night action, she overheard him talking trash into his cell phone in Arabic. He was in boss mode, barking demands and orders so she knew he had to be in a position of power. His walk, talk, dress, his whole demeanor screamed it. So she was caught off guard when he told her the homoerotic acts he wanted her to perform on him. Not to mention, she was surprised by the $5,000 dollars he offered her to do the things he wanted done. This entire scenario is why she always reminded herself to never judge a book by its cover. She lifted Omid's head back from her strap-on and said, "I'm not done with you yet, ho. Get your ass in that bathroom and get cleaned up." she harped up some phlegm and spat it in his face. The warm goo slid down the side of his face and went over his lips.

"Mmmmm," He scooped the glob from off his face and sucked it from his fat fingers like it was barbeque sauce.

"Oh, youz a nasty ass mothafucka," she said, sucking on her left breast's nipple. She smacked him on his ass as he hurried into the bathroom to freshen up. She then took a small copper key from her patent leather jacket, unlocked the padlock on her chess and lifted its lid. She removed a black leather bondage suit, a cache of sex toys, gadgets, lotions, oils and creams and lined them up on the dresser neatly.

Later that day

Omid disrobed and drew the shower curtain back, meeting a series of flashes from a photography camera.

"What the fuck?" He cursed, using one hand to block the flashes and the other to shield his privates. "Nightmare, who let you into my home?" he asked with a thick accent.

"I did," Bobby Blue said from the doorway, where she was clutching a sexy chrome, pearl handle .38 pistol with both hands. She pulled the Cleopatra wig off and tossed it on the floor. Beneath it she was wearing a wave cap over her hair, which was in cornrows.

"Fucking bitch!" Omid snapped, turning red in the face and around his neck. He was so pissed off that a vein began pulsating in his forehead.

"That's Queen Bitch to you," her eyebrows dipped and she twisted her lips, training her small caliber weapon on him. The end of the barrel of the gun gleamed once the light hit it.

"You must really have a death wish coming here," Omid barked on Nightmare without a trace of fear. Most men in his position would be shitting bricks, but he wasn't afraid to die. He embraced death. There was nothing to be scared of as far as he was concerned, dying meant starting life over from scratch to him. "What the fuck do you want?" He asked, wrapping a bath towel around his waist.

"The question isn't what I want, it's what are you willing to pay for what I have?" Nightmare asked, smiling evilly. "I have some photos of you in some very compromising positions. I have to tell you, fat man, these dirty lil' secrets wouldn't go over to well with your business associates. A man of your caliber hunched over with a twelve inch rubber dick being jammed up his brown-eye," He shut his eyelids and shook his head in shame. "You'd be the laughing stock of the underworld, and what about your folks? From what I hear, your people aren't too fond of homosexuals. Do you think they'd be cool with taking orders from a faggot? Fuck naw!" he answered his own question. "They'd probably have you killed. Now, tell me I'm not right?"

"Fuuuuuck!" Omid shouted, bringing his hands down his face. He pinched the bridge of his nose, and massaged his chin as he thought to himself. "Alright, cock sucker, you've got me by the balls here. What do you want for this to go away?"

"What cha got?"

"200k and four bricks of raw," He told him, sitting down on the commode's lid. "It's in the safe inside the floor of my closet."

"You might as well have told me you had two hundred grand and four bags of fertilizer. That coke you got is some old bullshit." Nightmare kicked him hard as fuck in his side causing him to holler out and clutched his aching ribs. "The fuck is the combo, Cuz?" he told the gangsta crip the combination to his safe and he sent Bobby to retrieve the goods inside of it.

"Baby, are we happy?" Nightmare called out to his lady, keeping his attention on Omid who was clutching his side, grimacing. Worry was plastered on his face and fear poisoned his heart. He wasn't sure if he could trust the gangbanger to uphold his part of the deal.

"Oh, we're verrryy happy, sweetie." Bobby called back out jovially.

A couple of minutes later she returned to the bathroom with a loaded pillowcase slung over her shoulder.

"Was everything there?" Nightmare inquired.

"Yep," she smiled with satisfaction. He gave her a nod and she spun around to Omid, lifting her .38. The chamber turned when she pulled the trigger, releasing a shot that went right through his thigh and echoed throughout the bathroom. The Middle Eastern drug lord fell off of the commode, clutching his thigh and howling in agony, face tightening feeling the fire in his limb.

Nightmare kneeled down to him and raised his chin with his finger to make sure he was looking him directly in the eyes before he began talking. "Heed my words, you tub of lard, if anything should happen to me or my bitch, those pictures are going to make it into the hands of your associates, capeesh?"Omid nodded yes as he gritted his teeth in pain, grunting his excruciation. "That a boy." Nightmare smiled pleasantly as he patted him on the cheek like a mafia wise guy. He then stood erect and exited the bathroom with Bobby in tow.

Nightmare could have easily rocked the fat man to sleep, but it would have brought a lot of heat down on him. The Middle Eastern drug lord's associates didn't trust the gangster crip one bit, so if Omid were to have gone missing, he would have been the first one they'd come looking for. Handling the situation this way was smart, with the photographs Nightmare could bribe Omid for whatever he wanted.

It was a cut throat game and only the most ruthless of men could win.

***

"Daddy, we're here," Bobby announced, shaking Nightmare from his dozing as she pulled into the Del Amo Mall Shopping Center's parking lot. She parked four rows down from Marshall's department store and executed the engine. Her man glanced at the digital clock in the dashboard, it was 2:29 P.M, one minute before he was supposed to meet the man who could be his new cocaine connection.

As soon as the digital clock struck 2:30 P.M, a black H2 Hummer on sparkling "28 inch chrome rims pulled into the parking stall five stalls down. Spanish music spilled from the cracked tinted windows of the hog along with heavy tobacco smoke. The driver side door swung open and the bodyguard stepped out, one designer shoe at a time. He closed the door behind him and surveyed his surroundings, keeping his hand inside of his suit near his pistol. Julio was a five foot seven Dominican cat with the complexion of a walnut and a left-eye that twitched. He had a pencil thin mustache and he wore his hair in a tapered fade. He was decked out in a purple fedora and suit. A crocodile belt held up his slacks and his feet adorned a pair of crocodile skin shoes.

Julio stepped around back and pulled the door ajar for his boss. An older Latin gentleman slid out from the confines of the backseat. He planted a snake skin shoe on the asphalt and pulled himself into view, adjusting his tie. Looking from left to right, he took pulls of his cigar. Smoke billowed from his nostrils as he spat what was left of the cigar to the ground and mashed it out under his heel.

Nightmare hopped out of the car and made a beeline to where the older gentleman stood. As he approached Julio moved into his path with his hand inside of his suit, ready to lay him down if necessary. The older gentleman waved him off and he stood aside.

"A dog shits…" the older man told Nightmare and then waited for his response.

"…But it doesn't shit long," the gangsta crip finished the password he was given over the phone.

"Nightmare?" the older man asked, trying to confirm who he was talking to.

"America's Nightmare," he corrected him proudly.

"Step into my office," The older man moved aside to let Nightmare crawl into the backseat of the Hummer. Once he had crawled inside, the older gentleman snapped his fingers; that was Julio's cue. The bodyguard handed Nightmare a folded up piece of tinfoil. When he unfolded the tinfoil there was a line of cocaine inside. He scooped some up into the long fingernail of his pinky and snorted it up his right nostril. He experienced an amazing sensation that made his eyes water. He blinked a couple of times than he scooped up some more and rubbed it on his gums, tasting it.

"Alright," Nightmare began, sniffing and wiping his nose. "I fucks with chu."

"Walk with me," the older gentleman smiled and nodded towards the mall's entrance.

***

Nightmare and his Spanish connect made their way through the mall side by side. They discussed business and held their hands over their mouths. Due to the connect's line of work he never knew when he was being followed, or

172

when the Feds were present. The Alphabet Boys had some of the best lip-readers in their employ, and with a pair of binoculars they could make out what you were saying on the moon. The connect had switched up cars twice before he made it to the indoor mall, but he was still taking extra precautions. It was better to be safe than sorry. No drug dealer wants the pressure of a thirty year bid hanging over his head.

"What do you purpose?" the older gentleman massaged his chin. He and Nightmare were negotiating.

"I was thinking, fifteen a key. Fifteen a block and I'll cop thirty at a time from you. I know you can show me some love with that." He spread his arms and angled his head, raising an eyebrow, hoping he'd fuck with him.

"Hmmm," he thought on it for a second, "Ok, but only because you're good friends with my god son. You've got yourself a deal."

"I never got cho name, O.G." Nightmare gave him a firm handshake.

"Tango."

Chapter Fourteen

That night

Lil' Gangsta sat on a leopard print couch, smoking a blunt and snapping his fingers to Marvin Gaye's *I'd rather be with you*. The song was on the oldies mix tape playing inside the PS4 that was lying on the floor beside the floor model "40 inch television set. Lil' Gangsta was holing up in Bellflower with some BBW named Shawna and her four kids in her Section 8 apartment. He was happy as hell because he had finally figured out his next move. He was going to move out to Lancaster. The rent out there was dirt cheap. He heard that you could get a three bedroom apartment for about $650 a month. After finding a cool little spot to lay his head he was going to hook up with this Mexican broad he was fucking with brothers. They were moving some serious weed down there and he was sure they'd give him a good price on a few pounds of Kush. He'd then get her to rent him a second apartment in her name. Next, he'd turn that into a trap and push weed out that bitch all day every day. That's how he'd make his living, as the neighborhood weed man. He and Maria would have a couple of babies and then they'd use some of the money he made from slinging weed to buy a house to raise their little family in. And then a few years on down the road, when the homies had forgotten about him snitching, he'd return back to the hood. *Yeah right!*

Everything would be all good then, Lil' Gangsta thought, smiling as if he had brainstormed a fool proof plan before taking pulls of his blunt. Seeing that he had an ounce of Kush left and no swishers to roll up with, he decided to make a run to the liquor store. He tucked his long nose .44

revolver into his waistband and snatched Shawna's car keys from the coffee table. The kids were gone with their father for the weekend and Shawna was sound asleep from the dick down he'd given her twenty minutes ago. So he didn't have to worry about her waking up any time soon and bitching about him running off in her car when he came back.

***

The elevator came to a stop on the parking garage floor. As soon as Lil' Gangsta stepped off of the elevator he heard pitter patter at his right. When he turned his head he locked eyes with a German shepherd. The beast tilted his head and glared up at him, snarling and growling. Lil' Gangsta's eyes lit up and he swallowed the lump of fear in his throat, slowly stepped backwards. The sudden barking of the dog startled him and he took off running in the opposite direction, heart threatening to explode it was beating so fast.

"Haa! Haa! Haa! Haa!" Lil' Gangsta continuously glanced over his shoulder as he hauled ass with the vicious dog on him like stink on shit. His forehead was shiny from sweat and he was breathing like he had a bad case of asthma. "Oh shit! Oh shit!" he repeated, seeing the hostile animal right on his heels. *Boomp!* He grimaced having ran into a parked Astro van and crashed to the ground. Peeling his eyelids open, he lifted his head from the asphalt and looked around. As he rubbed the back of his head he looked around expecting the dog to attack. But that mean bastard wasn't anywhere in sight. The scenery was silent save for the occasional car driving by on the upper level outside of the black garage gate.

"Grrrrrrrrr!" he froze where he was about to get up, and his entire body trembled. At this point and time he was on his hands and knees. Sweat dripped off the end of his brow.

He shut his eyelids for a moment and swallowed the ball of nervousness in his throat. Once he peeled his eyelids open, his eyes shot to their corners and he gasped. Slowly, his head turned to his rear and he found the German canine there. His head was tilted down and he was glaring at him, baring his flesh tearing teeth. Its growling seemed to grow louder and louder the longer it stood there.

Suddenly, Lil' Gangsta scrambled to his feet and took off running. He nearly slipped and fell but kept on running; trying to put as much distance between himself and the wild beast that was on his heels. Still in motioning, he continued to glance over his shoulder, terrified that the hound was going to make him his dinner. When he turned back around, he ran dead smack into what felt like a brick wall to him. Looking up, he saw a faceless man wearing a big hat that shaded most of his face. Lil' Gangsta's eyes widened and his mouth moved animatedly. He was scared

and didn't know what the fuck to say.

Snikt!

The machete sounded as it was unsheathed from somewhere within the recesses of The Ghost's trench coat.

The young nigga didn't have enough time to do anything but throw up a hand to shield his face. His face twisted up and he prayed for a quick death. That prayer would go unanswered.

Snikt!

"Arrrrrrrrr!" He threw his head back, shrilling like a victim in a horror movie. He brought his quivering head down and looked to his right; his hand had been completely severed. Blood squirted out from the stump uncontrollably, pelting the ground as well as his sneaker. When he looked down he saw his severed hand lying there beside his sneaker. The hit-man swung his machete back around and his nose came loose from his face, flying across the parking lot. Lil' Gangsta shrilled louder than before and grabbed the space on his face that his nose once was. Blood spilled from between his fingers and slicked his hand wet. When he took his hand away from his face it was met by the hit-man's blade once again, leaving both of his arms handless. His fearful eyes shot up to The Ghost and the killer's razor sharp weapon went across his neck. His head fell off to the side and he dropped to his knees, falling flat on his chest.

The Ghost whistled and Hank came stepping from around a car. He tossed the victim's severed hand up in the air towards him and he snagged it out of the air. The beast chewed on the fingers of the hand hardily as his master watched attentively. Next, the killer pulled out a fist full of green rat poison capsules and dropped them beside Lil' Gangsta's lifeless body. With the deed done, he wiped the machete's blade off on the arm of his trench coat and sheathed it. Once he took pictures of the corpse that he'd created, he walked off and whistled for his companion. The dog snatched up the severed hand it had been devouring and followed its master's lead.

Hours later

Black Jesus awoke in a cold sweat, panting out of breath from a nightmare. It was the same nightmare he had been having for the past five years now; the one where he was beaten, sodomized, paralyzed and left for dead in the woods. Every time he'd awake from the horrible experience, he'd be relieved that it was just a bad dream.

That's when he'd look over to the wheelchair beside his bed, and realize that his life was very much his reality.

Black Jesus wiped the sweat from his forehead with the back of his silk pajama sleeve. He looked over to the clock on the dresser; it was 1:00 A.M. He pulled his wheelchair to his bed and slid himself into the seat. After he was good and settled, he rolled over into the bathroom. Flipping on the light-switch, his heart nearly leapt from his chest when he saw The Ghost standing before him.

"Oh, fuck!" Black Jesus shouted, holding his hand over his heart "You scared the living shit out of me fantasma! How did you get in here?" The hit-man didn't utter a word, he was as still and mute as a mannequin. The big brim hat he wore shaded all of his face, except his mouth. That was all Black Jesus could see when the killer spoke.

"I took care of your rodent," he said, tossing a manila folder over into the drug lord's lap. Black Jesus opened the folder; inside there were three photographs of a deceased Lil' Gangsta laid the fuck out.

Bullet ran into the bathroom with just his boxer briefs on and a pistol dangling at his side. "You alright?" he asked Black Jesus.

"I'm fine. Look," he handed him the three photographs. As Bullet looked over the photographs a smile broadened his face.

"Downed that mothafucka, that's what the fuck I'm talking about." Bullet said, his eyes lingering on the last photograph.

"You did a good…" the rest of the sentence died in Black Jesus' throat, when he turned around and saw that The Ghost had vanished. He looked to the bathroom window and saw its curtains ruffle as a breeze blew in. He rolled himself over to the window and shut it; he then spun around to his little brother. Bullet was still looking over the photos.

"Burn those and get the fuck outta here," Black Jesus demanded. "I've gotta take a shit."

The next day

"So, what do you think about Lil' Gangsta?" Detective Ortiz asked his partner of thirteen years, as he took swigs of a Corona in between flipping the meat over he had cooking on the grill. He had a few guys from the force and their families over to his house for a barbeque. There were chicken, beef franks, beef patties, pork ribs and hotlinks going on the Black & Decker grill. There were ice cold beers and sodas on ice inside of the ice chess. While the adults mingled amongst each other, their children played in the pool.

"What about him?" Detective Arsenegger's forehead indented.

"You think he's ever going to show his face again?"

"No way, he definitely bailed. The little bastard hasn't answered the cell we gave him, and he has yet to report back. We should have never let that spade walk. If he hasn't skipped town by now, he's lying somewhere in a ditch, courtesy of his own homies." He took a swig of his Corona and savored the flavor.

"You know when he walked that Gangsta's conviction pretty much walked with him." Ortiz told him as he turned the meat over.

"If he does walk, we'll wait for an opening and pounce on his ass."

"How are we going to do that? When he got picked up his entire crew went AWOL figuring he'd use them to bargain his way out of prison. There's no one left to flip." Ortiz closed the lid on the grill and took a seat next to his partner, letting his Corona dangle in between his legs. "Then we'll go above and beyond the law. We'll go into our vigilante bag. We'll dead Gangsta, his nephews and their entire operation. That's the only way I can see this thing ending. I don't know about you, but I'm tired of playing this little cat and mouse game we got going with these clowns. It's time to kill them all and let the good Lord sort them out. All I want to know is that you have my back when the time comes." He looked Ortiz dead in his eyes, forehead furrowed and lips twisted. Determination twinkled in his pupils, causing them to look like crystals.

"Hey, am I, or am I not your dawg?" Ortiz raised his fist. Arsenegger smiled and gave him a pound.

"Aye, can a guy get a rib or something? I'm freaking starving over here!" One of the officers yelled out.

The crooked badges chuckled and went back to chopping it up, attending to the meat.

Chapter Fifteen

That night

"Damn, Blood, the crabs tried to straight up eighty-six you," Panic shook his head from the couch.

"I'm still tripping off of blood lying there playing possum," Woo said, munching on some Sunflower seeds.

"Avenue shoved me to the ground as soon as the shots went off. After they popped him, Blood threw his body over me to shield me. By the time I seen that crab nigga Nike coming, it was too late to pull my strap so I said fuck it and played dead."

All of the homies were accounted for except Debo and Neck Bone; they were busy holding down the traps.

"So, Blood saved your life?" Big Head asked from the sofa, looking higher than giraffe pussy.

"Yeah, he did, that's why we've gotta put the smash on these niggaz tonight," Pavielle said behind a murderous scowl, clenching his fists so tight that veins rolled around his knuckles.

"Word on the street is that Nightmare ordered the hit and sent Nike and Supacrip to carry it out," Panic informed his comrades. "Y'all already know what this shit is over, right?" he looked around to all of his comrades to make sure that he had all of their attention before answering his own question. "Turf…" he let it roll off of his tongue, "Since we got on them niggaz haven't been eating like their used to. What better way to solve the problem then to eradicate the competition?"

"Right," Panic nodded his understanding. "Kill the head and the body will follow."

The sound of a shotgun being racked drew everyone in the living room's attention. They turned around and found Gouch with the powerful weapon in his scarred, calloused hands. "Y'all ready to show these niggaz what the dub block gang is all about?" he looked them all in the face trying to find any reluctance to put in work.

"Two sho'," Panic said, catching the shotgun as Gouch tossed it to him. Once he caught it, he marveled it like it was a pretty fine thang with a big old ass, kissing it tenderly. *It was love at first sight!*

Gouch then went into the army sack by his feet and handed out guns to everyone in the living room except Pavielle. Being the leader of their organization, he didn't have to get his hands dirty; he had soldiers to go to war for him. The streets were about to feel his presence without him being there. That was for damn sure.

The young kingpin looked around the room at all of his homeboys; they were all examining their weapons and their magazines. He looked to the spot on the couch where Killa Dre was and he had vanished.

"Where that nigga Dre at?"Pavielle asked.

"What's up, Blood?" the young nigga spoke from the doorway; his eyes were bloodshot from the blunt he smoked with Big Head. He had been taking a piss while the others fraternized in the living room.

"You tryna get with these crabs that wet cha brother or what?" Pavielle asked, placing a firm hand on his shoulder, gripping it affectionately.

"Is it the fool that smoked my brother? Or is it just some niggaz from the other side?" Killa Dre lifted an eyebrow. He wanted the life of the killer that laid Tramel down, because to him that's the only way his sibling could rest in peace. "And please don't lie to me, big homie. I've been being lied to for as long as I can remember."

Pavielle thought for a second and blew hard, running his hand down his face. "I'm not going to lie to you, Duce Owe, I don't know if the fool that smoked your brotha is gonna be among this lot. But I promise you this; we will find the mothafucka that smoked your peoples."

"Put that on the gang." He looked him in his eyes.

"That's on the gang." Pavielle spoke with a seriousness that bled from his eyes.

"Alright."

They done a complex handshake and pounded the Blood 'B' against their chests.

***

Ponk!
Ponk!
Ponk!

The Spalding Basketball went as C-note bounced it on the asphalt, up and down. He and his road dawg, Crow, were passing through the hood when they spotted their little homeboys playing basketball in the street. C-note and Crow started reminiscing about their glory days on their basketball team back in high school. Each man swore he had a better jump shot than the other, so to settle the dispute they opted to play a game, best three out of five shots. The winner would receive $5,000 dollars plus bragging rights.

The $5,000 dollars was lunch money to the curly haired Belizean, C-note. He was one of the members of the three headed monster, each man was a millionaire. Crow wasn't sweating the five stacks either; he was C-note's right-hand man, so he was getting his slice of the American Dream, too. The homies had been competitive since grade school; one was always trying to outdo the other. So their little

183

game was more so about the bragging rights than the $5,000 dollars on the line.

Sweat dripped from C-note's brow as he bounced the basketball on the asphalt, his little homies on the edge in anticipation. One bit his bottom lip, another had his fists clenched, and the other had his hands together, silently praying. The three of them had their re-up money riding on the crip, so if he missed this shot they were fucked with a capital F.

C-note took a deep breath, lifted his arms and let the hog skin fly from his palms. The basketball appeared to being traveling in slow motion through the air. It bounced off one side of the rim, then the other, rolled around and fell into the basket.The little homies went wild and so did the shooter; he was all in Crow's ear wolfing big shit. The darker skinned man had a stupid look on his face when his homie snatched the fitted cap full of cash from his grasp.

"Gimmie my mothafucking money, nigga," C-note removed his two bankrolls and was just about to hand his little homies their winnings when the challenger spoke up.

"Fuck that shit, Cuz. Double or nothing," A scowling Crow spat. He was a sore loser and his demeanor screamed it. C-note looked to his little homies questioningly, wondering if he should double the bet or not. The young niggaz exchanged glances and looked to him, shrugging their shoulders. "Fuck you looking to them lil' niggaz for,

Loc? You were wolfing all of that shit, double or nothing!"

He produced another bankroll from deep within his pocket. "What's up? Y'all gone ride with your big homie one more time?" C-note asked his little homies, spinning the basketball around on his middle finger.

The little homies exchanged glances; the tallest one nodded his head, "Fuck it, Cuz, double or nothing, we're riding with chu."

"Yeah, C-note, you can take this nigga!" the skinniest one added.

"Bet 'em. We've got cho back, C-note!" the heaviest one chimed in.

"Old cheerleading ass niggaz," Crow shook his head shamefully.

"You got the lil' homies faded, Cuz?"

"Yeah, I got these lil' niggaz faded, 'cause when I'm done everybody out this mothafucka going home broke!" he swore, dropping his bankroll and the little homies fade into the cap as well.

The heaviest of the little homies shot past C-note.

"Where you going, nigga?" he called out after him as he spun the basketball on his middle finger.

"Over to these bushes. I gotta take a piss." Burger called out as he ran into the yard.

"Cuz, don't whip that lil' mothafucka out and cause C's momma to have a heart attack," a smiling Crow called out to Burger. All of the homeboys busted up laughing. Burger gave Crow the middle finger as he whizzed in the bushes.

C-note looked to his right and saw an idling Buick Regal in the middle of the block with its headlights out. A veteran of the streets and a highly decorated soldier, he already knew what time it was. "Enemies!" he yelled, dropping the basketball and going for his banger. The rest of the homeboys scrambled. C-note managed to pull his burner and fired two shots through the Buick's windshield, causing the glass to crack into several cobwebs. His eyes lit up as the car slammed into him and he traveled the length of the vehicle.

The door of the Buick Regal flew open and Panic, Woo, Big Head, Killa Dre and Gouch, all spilled out wearing bandanas over the lower halves of their faces. C-note laid strewn out in the street with a broken back moaning in agony, his arms and legs twisted at funny angles.

"Aaaah, my back," C-note cried in agony, his accent more evident now. "My mothafucking back, Cuz!"

"That's the least of your fucking problems, *Cuz*." Gouch rounded the trunk of the Buick pumping rounds into C-note's body as he passed him, blood speckling his Dickie's. The spent shell casings hit the ground dancing and making their own music. The killer then went off to join his comrades in the massacre they'd come to create.

Big Head ran up on Burger who'd just zipped up his jeans when he entered the yard. When the young nigga turned around and met the menacing eyes of his executioner, his eyes grew wide and he threw his trembling hands up into the air.

"Fuck your surrender, pussy!" Big Head blew a quarter size-hole through his chest and forehead, splattering his brains against the house. The mess there looked like spaghetti sauce as it dripped to the surface. He looked to his right and saw Panic chasing a shorter crip towards the backyard. Over his shoulder he caught Killa Dre and Woo chasing after a coal black crip, firing their weapons as they went along.

***

The tallest of the little homies hit the black iron-gate and had just about pulled himself over to the other side when his back exploded, sending atoms of shredded flesh and blood every where. He screamed in pain and fell down on his

186

back, grimacing and reaching for his wounded backside. Through teary eyes he saw a giant standing over him with the world's biggest shotgun pointed in his face. Right then and there, he forgot about his injury. He raised a bony hand in an attempt to plead for his life and his skull desentagrated, sending everything inside his head everywhere.

***

Killa Dre ran over the rooftops of cars lined up on the block in pursuit of Crow, while Woo chased after him on the ground. They breathed heavily and their faces wore coats of sweat as they relentlessly ran after their target. Crow dashed towards a main street. Seeing the well lit intersection with its passing automobiles and pedestrians gave him hope that he might live to see another day. He smiled broadly, but the expression on his face quickly converted to one of execruciation as his calf and kneecap exploded, spilling blood on the ground. He hit the asphalt like a stringless puppet, seeing Woo on one knee with his gun trained on him.

Crow lay in the middle of the intersection causing cars to nearly crash as they came to screeching halts trying not to hit him. As he bawled in pain Woo and Killa Dre ran up on him.

"Finish him, Blood," Woo told Killa Dre.

Gripping his Tec-9 firmly with both hands, Killa Dre held its trigger back, guiding the spitting machine up his target's groin and into his face. He released the trigger and his weapon wafted with smoke. He admired the bloody masterpiece he created, watching red streams flow from Crow's body.

187

Woo looked around and saw pedestrians and people inside of their vehicles watching them. "Come on, nigga!" he nudged Killa Dre and they ran off.

Chapter Sixteen

"So, who did y'all wet?" Pavielle asked as he sat down on the La-Z-Boy, holding his .9mm.

"C-note, Crow, and three other nobodies from their set," Woo told him. "We were tearing shit up out there."

"Blood, we caught them fools out there cold slipping." Killa Dre informed Pavielle excitedly. "It was just like you said, 'lay low for a minute, let'em think shit bool, and then pounce on their asses.'"

"I hope you wore something over your face. All it takes is one body for them boys to lock you up and throw away the key, ya Griff me?" Pavielle asked seriously.

"Yeah, all the homies wore something." Killa Dre nodded his head.

Pavielle looked over all of his homeboys' attire, they were all Cripped down. They were in Navy blue from head to toe: Chuck Taylor All Star Converses, Dickie suits, Pro Clubs, hoodies, fitted caps, beanies and bandanas. They donned these garbs to confuse the crips into thinking they were crips. Bloods who went on missions used this strategy sometimes.

"I had on this beanie, this flue rag and these shades," Killa Dre continued, holding up each item that he had called out. There was no way a civilian could identify him under his disguise. "Niggaz didn't bee Killa Dre from Outlaws smoke old boy in the middle of the street, they saw some crab nigga from some other crab set puff homeboy's wig out."

Pavielle smiled and gave the young nigga a pound.

"Y'all know it's about to be a full blown war out here now that y'all smoked one their shot-callers, y'all ready for this shit?" he asked, looking around at all of his comrades.

All of the homeboys nodded their heads. "Good. 'Cause the shits about to hit the fan," he rubbed his hands together and bit down on his bottom lip, anticipating the drama.

***

It was a gloomy Thursday morning when Nightmare came from the backyard with Karma on a blue leash. Stopping in the driveway, he fired up a Kush blunt; his breakfast for the morning, and looked over his hood. The dew had left the neighboring lawns slick and parked car windows fogged. People were leaving for work with their children in tow to drop off at school while others were returning home from their jobs.

Nightmare took a pull of his L and then blew the smoke into the cold air, watching it dissolve before his eyes. He then adjusted the straps in his waistband and moved to patrol his turf. Patrolling the neighbor-hood was something he and Karma did at 7:30 A.M every morning; rain, sleet, or snow.

He hoped to catch some enemies slipping while out on patrol. Normally he'd buck them down where they stood, but if he caught some out of bounds this morning he would sic Karma on them. It would be much more amusing to watch the pit chew his enemies up.

Nightmare smiled as the thought crossed his mind. *Yeaah, Cuz, I wish I would catch me a nigga slipping out here this A.M.*

A Lexus truck swung into the driveway of the house the gangsta crip was just about to cross. He went for one of his straps, but once it registered who it was inside the SUV he stayed his hand.

Nightmare's lieutenant and street son, Taco, hopped out of the truck. He was a skinny nigga who had a body that was a collage of tattoos. He wore his long hair in four thick

190

cornrows that hung passed his shoulders. He was twenty-one but didn't look a day over sixteen. With all his jewelry and designer clothes on the young nigga looked more like a rapper than a gangbanger.

Taco kneeled down and rubbed Karma behind her ears, the pit licked his face and hands as he did so. She considered the young hustler family just as her master did.

"How ya doing there, girl, huh? This nigga treating you right or nah?" he referred to her master before turning to him and giving him a pound. "What's cracking, Cuz?"

"You know, you almost got blasted on rolling up like that, right?" Nightmare frowned.

"My fault, homie, I need to holla at chu though, on some real shit." He stood in a half number four, with his fist inside the palm of his left hand. The look on his face was like *My nigga, you need to hear this shit,* but something else had caught his big homie's attention.

His sights were set on his little homie's ride. "Damn, Cuz, I must be paying you pretty goddamn good, you

rolling like that, Big Time?" he said, looking over Taco's diamond necklace as he held it in his hand, admiring the sparkling diamonds in the Jesus piece.

"Nike and Supacrip fucked up. They missed. That nigga Booby is still alive." Taco gave it to him raw and uncut. He said fuck it and decided to put it out there. "And a few of the homies got smoked last night." He added.

"Who?" Nightmare's brows furrowed and he blew smoke into the air.

"C-note, Crow and a few of the lil' homies."

"Mothafuckaz!" he looked away pissed off, placing his hand on his hip. Turning back around, he bowed his head and massaged the bridge of his nose.

"Your cell is dead or something?"

"Yeah, I forgot it in the car last night. The battery died. It's at the house right now charging."

"I had just got off the jack with the big homie Cas; he had been trying to get in touch with you. He wanna have a sit down with you tonight. He said for you to holla at him."

"Alright, you take care of that business for me?"

"Yeah, I had the workers break that shit down last night and bag it up. Shit is fire, too, Loc. We might be getting our custies back off of this shit." Taco nodded and rubbed his hands together greedily. A big ass Coca Cola smile spread across his face.

"For real?" Nightmare said, raising his brow.

"For real," Taco said, giving him a pound. Afterwards, they chopped it up for a time and then he made his departure.

Nightmare watched the back of the truck until it disappeared down the block. He couldn't help but thinking, *What the fuck does this nigga Cas wanna talk to me about?*

That night

Nightmare knocked on Cas's apartment door and moments later the door was pulled open by the double O.G. He wore a silk button-down shirt, matching pants and loafers. Gun held at his side, he gave his guests the once over before stepping aside to allow them to step inside. Once they were inside he closed the door behind them.

"Have a seat, make yourselves at home," Cas told them. "Would you like some apple cinnamon tea?"

"Nah, we good," Nightmare said, looking over the apartment, Cas's place was something else. It looked like it was an Asian Emperor's palace. If he didn't know the O.G lived there he would have sworn it belonged to a man of royalty. "You've gotta nice place here."

"Thank you," Cas grinned, laying his gun down on the counter and pouring himself a cup of apple cinnamon tea. Shutting his eyelids, he brought the cup to his nose and inhaled, taking in its tempting scent before taking a sip. A smile stretched across his face.

"What kind of incense you got burning in here, Butt Naked?" Nightmare inquired, loving the aroma that he'd gotten a whiff of.

"No, Black Love," He corrected him.

Leaning closer, in a hushed tone, Bobby said to her man, "What is he? A Muslim or something?"

"Five Percenter."

"You smoke?" Cas asked from the kitchen as he rummaged through the vegetable tray in the bottom of the refrigerator.

"Come on, Cuz, you know I smoke. My bitch does, too."

"Earth," the O.G frowned, annoyed by the gangsta crip referring to his lady as a *Bitch.*

"Huh?" Nightmare's forehead creased.

"Earth," he repeated himself. "You will refer to the sister by her name, or as Earth while in my presence, sun."

"Sure," Nightmare rolled his eyes. He wasn't trying to hear that shit. He knew that the O.G was deeply rooted with his religion and all, but he felt that he had belittled him in front of his woman. However, out of respect, he decided to hold his tongue on the matter.

Cas emerged from the kitchen with a big red ceramic bowl of Purple Kush buds, a five pack of grape Swishers Sweets in his shirt's pocket and his cup of tea. He sat the bowl on the glass table and tossed the box of blunt wrappers beside it.

"Would you do us the honor of rolling up, Mother Earth?" He asked Bobby. She told him sure and ripped the plastic off of the Swishers. She then removed them from their box and began rolling her first blunt expertly. Cas sat back and got comfortable in his seat before turning to

Nightmare, crossing his legs like a gentleman, "Now, about these red rags, I can see in your eyes that you have war on your mind, lil' brother."

"You fucking..." Nightmare cut himself short remembering how Cas didn't tolerate cursing in his home. "I mean, you're right. I want the slobs that killed my homeboys heads hanging over the fireplace in my crib." He replied honestly, eyebrows arched and lips twisted.

"I feel you on that, lil' brother," Cas took a sip of tea and savored the taste, licking his lips. "But starting up a war right now is only going to make the streets hot. The hood is going to be crawling with cops as soon as bodies start dropping, and with the pigs around, man, ain't nobody gone be out in the streets tryna cop no drugs. And that's gone fuck up the money."

"All your worried about is money, man?" Nightmare's eyebrows sloped and his nostrils pulsated.

"No, I care about our young brothers, too. But it's money over bull crap with me." He took another sip of tea, not giving a fuck about the gangsta crip being in his feelings. "We lost out on a lot of money since Booby entered the fold. I'm tryna see what this new product you got can do. If the stuff is as good as you say it is I'm sure we can get our ends back flowing right."

"Man, we're sitting on enough money between us to last until the beef is over. We're millionaires, Cas. I know you haven't forgotten, look how you living." He looked around at the lavish apartment and spread his arms wide.

"Lil'brother, you can never have enough paper, somebody told you wrong." He sat his cup of tea down on the coffee table and cleared his throat with a fist to his mouth.

"Man…"

"Look, the bottom line is, I'm not going to cosign your lil' war. So, if you go at these young brothers, man, you'll be going at them by yourself. Remember there are still two members of the three headed monster left, so you're going to need my go ahead before the brothers bear arms."

Nightmare lay back on the couch, blowing hard and running his hand down his face. He looked to Bobby who was licking the blunt closed and then to the O.G. "You know what, Cas? You're right. As long as you're still breathing, I can't handle this thing how I want to,"In a flash, he drew his chrome Desert Eagle and placed it to one of the fluffy couch pillows. "So, it's time you resigned."

Poof!

Poof!

Poof!

The couch pillow muffled the barks of Nightmare's banger as bullets tore through its suede fabric, knocking the stuffing out of it. Cas's belly exploded into a mass of blood, saturating the lower half of what he was wearing. His eyes doubled in size and his mouth quivered. He touched his wound and looked at his crimson stained palm, then back up at the gunman. He couldn't believe that Nightmare had shot him.

His eyebrows arched and his lips peeled back in a sneer. He went for the steel stashed in his pants and grabbed air. That's when he realized he had forgotten it on the kitchen counter. Cas got upon his feet and staggered towards the gangsta crip with his arms out stretched like a grizzly, roaring. Before he could reach him, Bobby came from his blindside and shattered a ceramic vase over his head. The O.G fell to the floor unconscious, Nightmare stepped over him. He placed a fresh couch pillow to the back of his head and pressed his banger in behind it. He pumped two rounds into the back of his skull like it wasn't nothing to him. He then stepped from over him and turned to Bobby. "Grab a towel and wipe down everything we touched. Do that now!" he ordered.

Bobby retrieved a washcloth and did as she was instructed. Afterwards, she and Nightmare turned the apartment upside down; once they were done the place looked like the police had raided it. They took Cas's stash, his flat-screens, and the few jewels he had. They then broke the chain on the door before they left the apartment. The plan was to make it look as if a couple of burglars broke into Cas's place, killed him and robbed him.

The next night

After the news of C-note, Crow, Cas and the little homies murders had spread like a wildfire throughout the hood. The homeboys were pissed off and thirsty for blood. They wanted some payback. Seeing his set anxious and eager to lay down some bodies, Nightmare called for a meeting in the backyard of his home.

"These slobs think something is sweet over here?" Nightmare asked his blue clad audience from the roof of his Cadillac. Bobby was sitting on the hood of the car filing her nails and chewing bubble gum. "These fools think they can pop two of our shot-callers and four of our homies and get away with it? They got me, nah, fuck that, they got *our* entire hood fucked up. Niggaz gone pay for touching ours! Oh, yeah, niggaz gone pay! That's on my dead daddy and my dead homies. I'ma ride, but I need to know my G's are with me." He looked over his audience, hoping to hear the voices of some brave souls.

"Yeah!" the audience answered in unison.

"Are y'all ready to bring it to these slobs?"

"Yeah!" the audience answered once more.

"I can't hear you," Nightmare said, cupping a hand behind his ear and leaning towards the audience. "Are y'all ready to bring it to these slobs?"

"Yeah!" the audience retorted as they fired their weapons into the air. They then chanted *Nightmare* over and over again. The gangster crip lifted his hands higher and higher into the sky, signaling to them to raise their voices higher. And they did.

There was about to be a lot of slow singing and flower bringing.

Chapter Seventeen

Nightmare had rallied his troops and so had Pavielle. With drive bys and walk-ups being executed on both opposing sides, bodies were dropping like flies and piling so high you could build a wall out of them. Pavielle was feeling the loss of every homie he lost but there was the death of one homie that really hit home for him.

Big Panic made his way out of Wally's Liquor Store with a brown paper bag in his hand. Its contents were a bottle of Alize, a box of Swishers, a box of Magnums and two clear plastic cups. The big man was overly excited; he had some ass on the line he had been trying to get for a month now. A little fine, educated honey by the name of Remy. He had been trying to get baby over to the house, but she seemed to always have an excuse. If she wasn't at school, she was at work, or taking care of her grandmother or babysitting her niece and nephew.

Panic was about to say fuck it and move along to this other broad he had bumped a week ago until he got a call from her out of the blue. He worked his charm and got her to agree to get a motel room with him. With images of her voluptuous, curvy body burned into his mental, he thought about how he was going to wax that ass like Mr. Miyagi. The thought alone had his dick nudging at the zipper of his jeans, trying to free its self.

Panic was so caught up in the XXX movie playing within the theater of his mind, that he hadn't spotted the two suspicious characters that had followed him in and out of the store. They had clung to the shadows and masked up with their chrome Uzis. When the big man went to stick his key into the key-hole of the driver side door, he saw their reflection in the window. His eyelids peeled wide open and his mouth formed an O as he gasped. The killers had their automatic weapons out stretched and were about to spray him. He whipped around quickly, dropping his bag of goods while in motion; he reached for the strap on his waistband. But it was far too late; the masked assassins already had the drop on him. Their Uzis fired in unison waking up the silent night as bullets struck their mark, misting the air with his blood. Panic danced on his sneakers as the bullets entered him and exited out of his back, splattering his blood against the side of his ride. It looked as if the bullets were attempting to levitate his three-hundred pound body from the surface. Panic crashed to the asphalt in the liquor store parking lot, landing hard on the ground. His blood ran from under him and mixed in with the alcohol that was concealed inside of the Alize bottle. The masked gunmen fled into the night, letting the darkness swallow them whole.

***

Pavielle lay in bed asleep beside Vayda. His cell phone's screen lit up and it danced across the nightstand as a call came through. The young kingpin stirred from his sleep and turned on the lamp light. He checked the caller I.D, pressed *talk* and brought the phone to his ear.

"What's up, Blood?" he asked groggily into the cell phone, wiping his eyes.

"Panic's dead." He spoke with a dead serious voice.

"Woo, it's too late at night to be playing, fam."

"I'm not playing, Bleed. Real spit, they hit'em tonight."

"Who?" Pavielle looked alive. His elevated voice stirred Vayda from her sleep. She narrowed her eyelids as she looked at him. By the look on his face she could tell something was terribly wrong.

"Nike and Supacrab," Woo told him, his voice slightly cracking under his emotions. "On Lil' Face it's on now,

Blood, me and Big Head 'bout to murder every last one of these niggaz. Dinosaurs ain't gon' be the only mothafuckaz that's extinct, on the set."

"Y'all chill for a sec," Pavielle began, sitting up in bed, "I'm a sic old girl on lil' homie. I'ma call her in the

A.M and get the ball rolling, alright?"

"Alright, Blood. I love you, my nigga."

"I love you, too, Duce Owe. Twenty minutes." he disconnected the call.

"Boo, what happened?" Vayda asked concerned, scratching her chest as she peered through narrowed eyelids.

Pavielle shut his eyelids and put his hands together in prayer, having a moment of silence for Big Panic. When he peeled his eyelids open, his eyes were glassy and attempting to accumulate tears. Seeing the hurt in her man's eyes, Vayda sat up in bed and took him by the face staring into his eyes. "Babe, tell me what's wrong, what happened?" she inquired, looking as worried as ever.

"My best friend was murdered tonight." He told her, and as soon as he spoke the tears jetted down his cheeks. He shut his eyelids for a moment and bit down on his bottom lip, nostrils flaring.

"Panic?"

"Yeah, go back to sleep, baby." He kissed her on the forehead and then cupped her face, kissing her on the lips. He then turned off the lamp and rolled over to go back to sleep, his heart heavy with grief.

***

Killa Dre scaled the fence of Inglewood cemetery high and drunk out of his mind. Jumping down to the other side, he staggered forward and fell to all fours. Slowly, he got to his feet searching his person. He was relieved that he hadn't dropped the 40 oz of Olde English malt liquor, but when he searched his ear for his half smoken blunt and discovered he'd lost it, he was disappointed.

"Shit!" he cursed.

Wide eyed, his eyes scanned the grounds for the blunt he'd dropped. When he didn't see it, he shut his eyelids and took a deep breath. "Fuck it." He ran his hand down his face and pulled his bottle of cheap alcohol from where he had it stashed. After twisting off the cap, he took it to the head, guzzling it. The bubbles floated to the bottom of the bottle as his throat rolled up and down his neck. Taking the 40 from his lips, he wiped his mouth with the back of his fist. Shortly thereafter, he shuffled forward drunkenly. Using the illumination from his cell phone, he searched the cemetery's grounds until he found his deceased brother's grave stone. Coming across it, he put his cellular away and stepped to it.

"'Sup with it, big bro?" He took the 40 oz to the head, guzzling it and pouring some on the lawn below his brother's marble stone. Having screwed the cap back on his alcoholic beverage, he went on to talk to his late sibling. Once he wrapped up their conversation, he made him a promise that he was definitely going to keep.

"The next time you see me here, big bruh, I'll have your killer's blood on these hands," he held up his hands and looked between them. After balling them into fists, he focused his attention back on the stone with his brother's name carved in it. "I swear to God...," his vision was quickly obscured by the tears that accumulated in his eyes, outlining the rims of them. The teardrops fell, hitting the grass and the tip of his right sneaker. "No," he sniffled and snorted back some of the tears that wanted to fall. "No, I swear to *you*, I'ma kill that nigga."

Thunder rumbled and lightening flashed, hiding his face in darkness and then revealing it, each time it made an appearance. Suddenly, rain fell from the sky looking like falling crystals. Killa Dre threw on the hood of his jacket and sat the Olde English bottle down beside his big brother's marble head. Stashing his hands in his pockets, he turned around and trekked back from where he came.

The next morning

"Thank you." Black Jesus said to his maid, Marisol, as she sat his breakfast and his cup of coffee down on the table before him. He slipped on his glasses and opened up the news paper, reading over it. The doorbell chimed, but he didn't bother to tell Marisol to answer it. The paper held all of his attention. Besides that, he already knew she'd get it, because it was just one of the tasks that he was paying her to do. Although he was focused on his reading, that didn't stop him from over hearing the locks being undone on the front door and the maid greeting Tango as he crossed the threshold.

"Jesus Christ, are you, okay?" he overheard her. This caused the drug lord to frown. He folded his paper in half and set it aside.

"I'm fine," he heard Tango say as he made his way through the living room. "Where's the jefe?"

"In the kitchen."

Black Jesus turned around just in time to see his bodyguard making his way toward him. He looked like he'd been through hell, and back and his arm was in a sling. When he saw this, he immediately thought, *Oh, shit.* The old gangster didn't even have to say it, because right then he already knew that his shipment had been hit.

Black Jesus' face balled up and he removed his glasses, sitting them aside on the table. He glared at Tango and said, "I wanna know who hit my shipment, and I wanna know now. So you for damn sure better have a name for me."

Tango nodded and said, "I do…Booby."

To Be Continued…

Me and My Hittas 2

AVAILABLE NOW BY TRANAY ADAMS

The Devil Wears Timbs 1-7

Bury Me A G 1-5

These Scandalous Streets 1-3

A South Central Love Affair

Me and My Hittas 1-6

The Last Real Nigga Alive 1-3

God Bless the Trappers 1-3

A Gangsta's Empire 1-4

Fangeance

Fear My Gangsta 1-5

A Hood Nigga's Blues

The Realest Killaz 1-3

The Last of the OGs 1-3

The Streets Don't Love Nobody 1-2

The Dopeman's Bodyguard 1-2

King of the Trenches

www.ingramcontent.com/pod-product-compliance
Lightning Source LLC
Chambersburg PA
CBHW070352200726
48294CB00003B/869